TiM POSSiBLE

& the Secret of the Snake Pit

Also by AXEL MAISY

Tim Possible & the
Time-Traveling T. Rex

Tim Possible &
All That Buzz

Tim POSSiBLE
& the Secret of the Snake Pit

· Axel Maisy ·

ALADDIN
New York   London   Toronto   Sydney   New Delhi

ALADDIN

An imprint of Simon & Schuster Children's Publishing Division
1230 Avenue of the Americas, New York, New York 10020
First Aladdin hardcover edition December 2023
Copyright © 2023 by Alexis Bautista Pradas
All rights reserved, including the right of reproduction in whole or in part in any form.
ALADDIN and related logo are registered trademarks of Simon & Schuster, Inc.
For information about special discounts for bulk purchases, please contact
Simon & Schuster Special Sales at 1-866-506-1949 or business@simonandschuster.com.
The Simon & Schuster Speakers Bureau can bring authors to your live event.
For more information or to book an event contact the Simon & Schuster Speakers Bureau
at 1-866-248-3049 or visit our website at www.simonspeakers.com.
Cover designed by Karin Paprocki
Interior designed by Mike Rosamilia
The illustrations for this book were rendered digitally.
The text of this book was set in Avenir Next.
Manufactured in the United States of America 1023 BVG
2 4 6 8 10 9 7 5 3 1
Library of Congress Control Number 2023933141
ISBN 9781534492752 (hc)
ISBN 9781534492769 (ebook)

To my parents,
ENI and FRANCISCO,
who love without condition
and give without expectation

MEET THE HEROES

This is Tim Sullivan. He drank Oskar's IMPOSSIBLE JUICE™, and now all his worries turn into reality. That's kind of dangerous because Tim worries. All the time. Like, a lot.

We're doomed. We're sooo doomed. . . .

Jajaja, vamos, bring it on!

You mean unpredictably "fun," right?

This is Tito Delgado. He reads comic books and laughs in the face of danger.

This is Oskar. He is a *T. rex*. And an unpredictable time-traveling genius.

THIS STORY

You know Tim and Tito. They're best friends. But if you've forgotten, Tim is the kid fleeing on the left, with the big eyes and the spiky hair. Tito is the kid fleeing on the right, with the mushroom cut and a half-chewed bocadillo bite in his mouth. And you might be wondering: Why are they running away like plump turkeys on Thanksgiving eve?

Meet the weremoles, an army of hungry, sharp-toothed rock-munchers looking forward to adding a side of fourth grader to their soily diet.

How did this happen? Will Tim and Tito end up being caught by the voracious hole-diggers?

Will they end up covered in more holes than a Swiss cheese? Can they dig themselves out of this terrible hole? And what about their time-traveling dinosaur friend? Could he be their ace in the hole?

Those are all fantastic questions with a whole lot of holes, but to answer them, let's restart this story. . . .

PART 1

HEROES AND VILLAINS

CHAPTER 1
THE BEGINNING

··· SUNDAY ···

Tim's life was complicated. His pet was a green half-pug, half-pickle hybrid, his neighbor was a troublemaking time-traveling dinosaur, and ever since he'd drunk the IMPOSSIBLE JUICE™, his worries had enough power to end the galaxy. But on that Sunday afternoon, as he walked down the street with the late-spring sun's warmth tickling his cheeks, Tim couldn't help but smile.

He'd just had the most wonderful time walking Puckles in the park . . . alongside Zoe and her pug! They had chatted, they had laughed, they'd even shared earphones! Tim was on cloud nine. Zoe Charms was the coolest, loveliest, most popular fourth grader in town, and somehow, inexplicably, they'd become great friends.

Things were looking up, or so Tim thought . . . right until he stepped into his backyard and found that it'd been transformed into a wild ninja-warrior-worthy obstacle course!

PHOOEY! He'd forgotten that today was his first day of superhero training. He should've met Tito and Oskar hours ago! It was bad. *Really* bad. His friends had been planning this for weeks. How could it have slipped his mind?

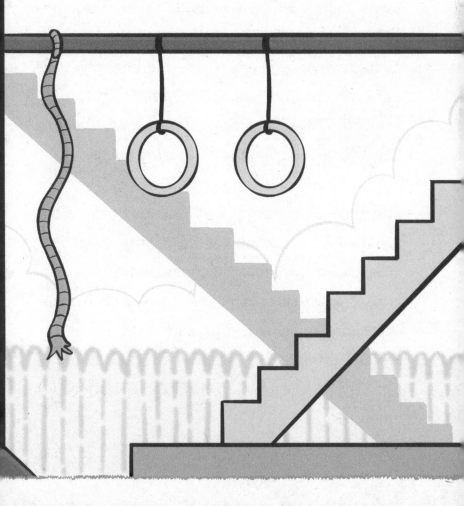
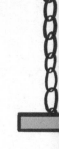

With a mix of shame and awe, Tim scanned the sprawling maze of climbing walls, balance beams, hanging rings, poles, pits, pools, rope bridges, and swinging platforms that his friends had built just for him. A tight knot formed in his chest. Tito and Oskar had both put in a ton of work to help him, and he hadn't even shown up. The guilt was unbearable. *WHAT IF they think I'm a terrible . . . ? WHAT IF they never forgive . . . ?* The moment Tim's stomach started to flutter, he closed his eyes and took a deep breath. *Breathe in. Breathe out. Breathe in. Breathe out.*

You see, over the last few weeks, Tim had become increasingly good at preventing his worries from getting out of control, thanks to the use of breathing techniques and mindful observation. But even as he calmed down, one certainty remained: *Tito and Oskar must be terribly upset!*

"That was epic! Can we do this again soon, please?"

"Sure! Sure!"

Tim's thoughts were interrupted by the sounds of Tito's and Oskar's voices. He turned around. He was ready to face his friends' anger and to beg for their forgiveness. However, he wasn't ready for what he saw. Why on earth did Tito and Oskar look like bananas?

"Hey, look, it's Tim!" said banana-Oskar.

"¡Hombre! Where were you?" asked banana-Tito, patting Tim on the back. "You missed all the fun. We just returned the monkeys!"

Tim stared at his fruity friends, confused. *Er...monkeys? Bananas?* "Wh-wh-what's going on?"

Oskar and Tito shared a look that Tim couldn't quite understand, and then they broke into laughter.

"It was supposed to be part of your training," explained Oskar. "I thought that the obstacle course would get boring after a few tries, so I brought my Foodifier 3.0 to turn you into a giant banana, and two hundred hungry monkeys to chase after you."

Tim shuddered. What sort of training was that?

"But since you were nowhere to be found and the monkeys were getting restless, we decided to give it a try ourselves," said Oskar.

"You should've seen us. IT WAS AWE-SOME!" added Tito. "I can't remember the last time I laughed so hard! Anyway, what happened to you?"

Tim's face reddened. "I kind of . . . forgot." He looked down and swallowed hard. "I was with Zoe. She called earlier today." Tim paused. "I know I let you down. I'm sorry."

Oskar chuckled. "Relax! It's fine! The two of us had so much fun. Right, Tito?"

Tim watched his friends laugh and tease each other. They'd bonded during his absence, that much was clear. He should have been happy that they weren't mad at him, and yet . . .

WHAT IF they start hanging out together and leave me all by . . . ?

"I have an idea," said Tito, perhaps noticing that Tim was feeling left out. "Why don't you ask Zoe to join us next time? Together we'll teach those monkeys a lesson!"

Tim forced a smile. "Sure, I'll ask her . . . next time." He tried his best to sound like he meant it, but he didn't. How was he supposed to ask Zoe if she wanted to be turned into a banana so a horde of hungry monkeys could chase after her? The moment Zoe heard that, she would run for her life and never look back! And let's face it, could he blame her? Likewise, Tito and Oskar would get bored by the things that Zoe and he liked to do. NO. Tito, Oskar, and Zoe didn't belong together, so mixing them up was a recipe for disaster. He wouldn't do it. He couldn't! He didn't have friends to spare.

CHAPTER 2
FRIENDSHIPS ARE HARD WORK

··· MONDAY ···

When Tim left home the following morning,
his eyes burned with the fire of determination.
The plan was clear: the only way to protect
his friendships was to become the best friend
anyone could wish for. He couldn't afford to
make any more mistakes. He was going to be

there 100 percent for Tito, 100 percent for Oskar, and 100 percent for Zoe, too.

The first class of the day was a pet first-aid workshop taught by Ms. Fangs, the school nurse. She brought in a couple dozen fluffy chinchillas, and each of the students got to choose one to practice the basics of pet care. Tim couldn't have asked for a better bonding activity. He shared some laughs with Tito, and then some more with Zoe, and he would've spent some quality time with Oskar, too, if the dinosaur hadn't been too busy having a heated argument with his chinchilla.

Next came Music of the World with Ms. Mamba. Tim, keenly aware of the need to be close to his friends at all times, expertly maneuvered himself and his five-foot-long didgeridoo into a strategic spot, with Tito on his left, Zoe on his right, and Oskar right behind him. *Easy!*

Things were going well—or as well as they could go with twenty fourth graders playing twenty different instruments at the same time—when Ms. Mamba threw Tim the first curveball of the day.

"Thank you, that sounded lovely," she said, motioning for everyone to stop. "Now please find a partner and play a duet."

A partner? Tim's brain went instantly into overdrive, considering the possible pairing scenarios and their potential consequences for his friendships. Partnering with Tito seemed the obvious choice since:

1. They always did everything together,
2. Oskar wouldn't mind—he never paid any attention in class anyway, and
3. Zoe was so popular and had so many other choices that she probably wouldn't even consider partnering with him.

It was decided. Tim turned to the left and raised an eyebrow, and Tito answered with a thumbs-up. And so, without a single word being uttered, Tim got his partner.

Or not. Tim heard his name being called on the right.

"Hey, Tim, would you like to play with me?" whispered Zoe.

Tim's heart skipped a beat. That was terrible timing! And yet . . . This was the first time ever that Zoe had asked him to be her partner. It was a key moment in their friendship; he couldn't let it go to waste! He had no choice but to stick to the plan. "Sure?" he whispered back.

Did Tim then turn around and tell Tito that he was partnering with Zoe instead? Don't be silly, of course not! He couldn't risk losing his best friend! Instead Tim took a big breath and began blowing on the didgeridoo as if his life depended on it. Tito joined with his maracas on the left. Zoe joined with her Chinese erhu on the right. And by some miracle, they each thought that Tim was playing with them. *Please don't let them find out. Please don't let them find out,* Tim prayed in silence, while he waited for the dismissal bell to ring. Five very long minutes passed, and finally, **RIIIIIING!** Tim let out a sigh of relief. It had worked! The crisis had been averted.

That wasn't the end of Tim's troubles, though. Because after thanking Zoe for helping him put away his giant instrument, he blurted, "By the way, are you doing anything during recess?"

CHAPTER 3
FIRST RECESS

Tim immediately regretted asking that question. What was he thinking? He spent every recess with Tito and Oskar. Twice a day, midmorning and noon, they sat at the same table in the cafeteria and they ate, chatted, and had a great time. It was their thing, their time, a sacred pillar of their friendship. So what was the point of asking Zoe if she was free?

It sounded as if he were inviting her to join them. And then what? He couldn't say no; it might hurt her feelings. But wasn't the plan precisely to avoid Tito, Oskar, and Zoe getting together? Tim held his breath and braced for the worst.

"Sorry, I have a meeting with the Leadership Club to work on the Summer Parade," said Zoe.

"There's lots to do, so we even got permission from Mr. McWriggle and Ms. Conda to skip their classes."

That's right! thought Tim. Zoe was the busiest girl in the whole school: sports, clubs, committees, she was involved in them all. Thank goodness for that! He relaxed, confident that the danger was gone, until Zoe added, "I could join you for lunch recess if you want, though!"

INSIDE TIM'S HEAD

GO! GO! GO!

MAYDAY! MAYDAY! WE HAVE A PROBLEM! Tim remained silent, but inside his head sirens were blasting. A few weeks ago, he would've sold a kidney to hear Zoe utter those words, and yet, right now, as he was hearing them, all he could think of was ways to pretend it'd never happened. How on earth was he going to get out of this mess without hurting any of his friendships?

Tim was sweating buckets. "I . . . well . . . lunch . . . yes . . . you see . . ."

"It would have to be a bit later, though," added Zoe. "I have track practice till twelve thirty. Would that work for you?"

Tim's eyes popped wide open. There it was: an opportunity! He could eat lunch twice! First in the cafeteria with Tito and Oskar, and then he could come up with an excuse and . . .

"In that case, why don't we eat on the bleachers by the athletic field?" asked Tim. "I can bring some sandwiches from the cafeteria."

He grinned. Yes, Tito and Oskar would never find out. That could work!

Zoe laughed. "Like a picnic? It's a deal. I love it!"

A few minutes later, in the cafeteria, Tim chewed a cereal bar mindlessly while Tito and Oskar reminisced ONCE AGAIN about the fun they'd had the previous day. Was there no other topic? One he could add to? Tim's stomach growled. Tito and Oskar were already ignoring him! Perhaps it would be a bad idea to leave them halfway through lunch recess. *WHAT IF . . . ?*

CLICK! The lights in the cafeteria went off, and a giant spotlight lit up the main door. A slow-moving fog started to pour into the cafeteria from the hallway. *What now?*

"I think someone's about to make a grand entrance," said Tito.

Suddenly the first notes of an epic guitar riff screamed through the school's PA system, and a deep voice, just like the one in action-movie trailers, announced the mysterious visitor:

"In a world full of darkness, there's a sparkling ray of hope. A true superhero. A shining beacon of justice. The one and only . . ."

CHAPTER 4
DIAMOND BOY!

The music raged, there was a loud BANG!, and as the lights came back on, a kid stormed in through a cloud of confetti, waving and high-fiving left and right. The cafeteria exploded in cheers, but Tim gasped in disgust.

It was *him*! Tim's nemesis, the always-snotty-and-rich-beyond-measure kid who had almost succeeded in making Tim the most hated student in school. The spoiled brat who had put humanity in danger and somehow had still managed to steal all the credit for Tim's heroic actions.

Meet Diamond Boy. The not-at-all-secret alter ego of William Woodrow Wiggle the Third (also known as W).

That slimeball was no superhero!

W stood on an empty table. He was wearing a skintight bodysuit covered in real diamonds, and every move he made filled the entire room with sparkles.

"Thank you, thank you, you're too kind," he said, in his usual high-pitched voice. "Am I a superhero? I don't know. I mean, look at me, what do you think?"

Tito sneered and leaned toward Tim. "I think that he looks like a walking disco ball."

Tim held back a giggle.

"Anyway, I came here today to make two big announcements," continued W. "The first one has to do with this," he said, pointing to a camera that he was wearing on a head strap. "This whole week I'll be recording everything I do, and I'll be streaming it live on Glitch!"

W stopped as if he were waiting for applause. However, the room remained silent. The boy cleared his throat.

"But hold on. My second announcement is even bigger!" he said, drawing out a diamond-encrusted flyswatter and pointing it at the ceiling. "As you might remember, it was I who single-handedly saved the world from being taken over by insects."

You wish, thought Tim, rolling his eyes.

"And yet, there're still bugs everywhere!" W added. "So I ask you, How can we be sure that they won't attack us again?" He paused and stared at his audience. "WE CAN'T!"

"The enemy lives among us, but don't fret!" the kid continued. "Starting today, I'm taking on the responsibility of chasing those buggers out of town to keep you all safe!" The annoying kid used his fancy flyswatter to draw the shape of a

W midair, and the cafeteria burst into applause.

Tim frowned. "What a nitwit!" he whispered, drawing an assenting nod from both of his friends. If only people knew the truth: W was most to blame for the insect uprising, not the poor critters themselves!

Bugs could actually be quite nice. Tim sighed at the memory of Margot, his former pet fly turned giant exiled hero. He missed her. *I wonder how she's doing. . . .*

"I'll be leaving now, but please keep your eyes open and report to me any insect you find sneaking around," W said. "I, Diamond Boy, your humble protector, will take care of it!"

Without any warning, Oskar stood up, pointed at W, and yelled at the top of his lungs:

I'm seeing a huge shiny dung beetle standing on a table right now!

CHAPTER 5

SUPER FRIENDS

Tim almost passed out. What was Oskar thinking? The last thing they needed was to get in trouble with W once again! But even though the *T. rex* rolled on the floor, laughing his tail off, no one, not even W, paid him any attention.

Are you surprised? Don't be. Oskar never leaves home without putting on his Pulverized Odor Ordinarifier 5.0, a high-tech spray-on perfume designed specifically to make him look ordinary no matter what!

It wasn't until W left the cafeteria that Tim began to calm down. "That wasn't funny, you know," he scolded Oskar.

Tim wasn't being completely honest, though. Now that the fright was past, the scene seemed a whole lot funnier. So much so that he added, "Also, for the record, W is stinkier than any dung beetle!"

The three friends shared a good laugh.

"Seriously, I don't get it!" said Tim. "How can anyone in their right mind believe that W saved the world? Can't they tell that his only superpower is being super rich?"

"Thaph's noph all," corrected Oskar, swallowing a mouthful of pickles. "He's super annoying, too!"

Tim chuckled. It was hard to believe: Oskar's jokes were actually improving!

"Here's an idea," said Tito, who had been

silent for a while. "Why don't WE create our own superhero team?"

Tim stared at Tito, trying to decide if his friend was joking. No, he wasn't. Ever since Tim had drunk the IMPOSSIBLE JUICE™, Tito was convinced that Tim could become a superhero. Tim, however, wasn't so sure. "We need to be realistic," he said. "I might never be able to control my power. Right now the best I can do is keep my worries in check and hope that I don't create another mess. And let me tell you, even that is a struggle!"

Tito smirked. "Tim, Tim, Tim. Sometimes I think I know you better than you know yourself. Mark my words: one day, sooner or later, you'll be in control of your worries. I have no doubt about it. Perhaps if you start showing up for superhero training, you'll begin to understand why."

Tim blushed.

"However, I'm not talking about your power

right now," Tito added. "Reading comic books has taught me that we don't need superpowers to become superheroes. Look at Batkid and Robin!"

"Right, but Batkid happens to be a gazillionaire, just like W, and you and me, we have no money!" insisted Tim.

"That's true, but we have something way

better than money," said Tito, pointing a finger to his immediate right.

It wasn't hard for Tim to figure out what his friend was getting at. He wanted them to use Oskar's inventions—which, by the way, had already almost destroyed the world twice—to become crime-fighting vigilantes. It was the most terrible idea Tim had heard in a while! It was so terrible, and so terrifying, in fact, that just thinking about it was giving him a stomachache. *Breathe in. Breathe out.*

Tim's first instinct, logically, was to speak his mind and say no. However, the excited glint in Tito's eyes gave him pause. What if he said no, and his friends decided to do it anyway without him? Tim's stomach rumbled. Tito and Oskar had already found out that they could have lots of fun on their own, so the possibility wasn't out of the question. NO. He couldn't risk it! If being the perfect friend required him to set his better judgment aside, then so be it!

"That's . . . brilliant!" he lied.

"I knew you'd like it. ¡Vamos!" said Tito.

"Lepht's do itph!" cheered Oskar.

And that's how on that sunny spring morning, Metrosalis's first and only superhero ensemble team was born.

CHAPTER 6

THE JUSTICE THREE

Meet the Justice Three:

He has the power to make the impossible happen, but he never uses it.

He is an unpredictable genius and a time-traveling *T. rex.*

He is brave and strong, and knows everything about sandwiches and comic books.

"What should be our first order of business?" asked Tito, grinning from ear to ear. "Superhero names?"

Tim shook his head. "I think we should stick with our real names for the time being."

"You're right, you're right." Tito nodded. "Our top priority should be to find something heroic to do. A superhero without a crisis is just a weirdo in a cape, which, by the way, reminds me . . ."

NO! We're not wearing capes either!

AW, MAN!

"Let's focus on finding a fun mission," said Oskar. "My life has been awfully quiet since a certain someone learned to ignore his worries."

Tim rolled his eyes.

"Actually, I have one suggestion," said Tito. "Why don't we try to reveal the evil hiding in our school once and for all?"

Tim smiled, pleasantly surprised. Perhaps the Justice Three was not such a bad idea!

You see, Leaping Cobra Elementary School (LCES) was not an ordinary boring-run-down-dreary kind of school. On the contrary, it was about the nicest place on the entire planet. It had a nice building, with nice computers on nice desks inside nice classrooms. It had a nice cafeteria run by three nice ladies that served nice French food every second Friday. It had a nice gym, a nice science lab, and five different nice playgrounds that were open all year long for everyone's enjoyment. It was really nice. Super nice. So nice, in fact, that Tim and Tito had always suspected that it was all a cover for a sinister secret.

It was time to find out the truth. And both Tim and Tito knew where to start looking.

MS. CRAWLEY!

If LCES was a cesspool of evil, then Ms. Crawley—LCES's cheerful, smiley, and always-incredibly-nice principal—was its evil mastermind.

Oskar didn't share his friends' suspicions, though. "That sounds like a giant waste of time," he said. "Our school is perfectly fine, and as far as I can tell, Ms. Crawley truly cares about her students."

"That's because she's really good at keeping up appearances!" argued Tim.

"Yes," agreed Tito. "We need a way to get close to her when she thinks that no one's looking. That's when we'll get to see the real her. Do you have anything that could help us?"

Oskar shrugged. "I could use my Foodifier 3.0 to turn you into some snacks," he suggested. "How would you like to become walking cookies? That could be fun to watch!"

Tim threw his hands into the air. "How on earth do you expect a couple of walking cookies not to stand out?" he asked in exasperation. "We're looking for a device that allows us to remain unnoticed while we spy on Ms. Crawley, like flies on the wall."

"A drink that turns us into stealthy ninjas, perhaps?" said Tito.

"Or a cloak of invisibility," suggested Tim. "That would work too."

Tim and Tito wearing a cloak of invisibility

Oskar didn't seem to be listening anymore. "Flies on the wall, eh?" he mumbled, rubbing his chin. "Yes, I think I have something back home that you could use. I'll go fetch it! Meet me outside, behind the greenhouse, at noon."

Tim gasped. "Noon? As in TODAY'S noon?" He swallowed hard. "Isn't that too soon? Why don't we leave it for another day?"

"Why? Are you busy today?" asked Tito.

Yes! thought Tim. *I'm supposed to be meeting Zoe at twelve thirty!* He couldn't admit that to Tito and Oskar, though. "Well . . . I . . ." He hesitated. He hadn't come up with a good excuse yet! What should he do? "I . . . I guess I'm not," he lied.

"Then it's settled," said Tito. "We'll put our plan into action during lunch recess!"

Tim closed his eyes and massaged his temples. This stress was giving him a headache! *Breathe in. Breathe out. Breathe in. Breathe out.* The flutter in his stomach eased a bit. *There's no need to freak out, Tim. Thirty minutes should be plenty of time to spy on Ms. Crawley, shouldn't it?*

A hand landed on Tim's shoulder. "You seem tense," said Tito. "Relax! In less than two hours we'll show the world what real superheroes can do. It's going to be awesome!"

On his way out, Oskar turned around and smiled. "Oh yes, it most definitely will. . . ."

CHAPTER 7
FLIES ON THE WALL

Flies? Seriously?

Two hours later, behind the school's greenhouse, Tim buzzed around Oskar's head angrily. "STOP LAUGHING AND CHANGE ME BACK! THIS WASN'T PART OF THE PLAN!"

Oskar sat on the ground in tears. "What do you mean? It was your idea! Didn't you want to become flies on the wall?"

What Tim wanted was to scream. He'd been so wrapped up in his own problems that he'd missed the signs. He should've known that the way Oskar had smiled when he'd handed them his invention had meant trouble. Tim should've asked what "F.O.T.W. 3.0" stood for. He should've, but he hadn't, and now he had six legs, big red eyes, and a pair of wings. How was he going to have lunch with Zoe looking like this?

"It's fine, Tim," said fly-Tito, twisting in the air like the world's smallest fighter jet. "This camouflage is exactly what we need!"

"If that's all, you should get going. You have important buzz-iness to attend to!" teased Oskar. "And, Tim, don't worry. I'll return you to your human forms as soon as you come back."

At those words, Tim relaxed a bit. As long as they got this spying business over with fast, he'd be able to meet Zoe. "Okay, Tito, let's get this done!"

Unfortunately, being flies in a school that had recently declared war on insects complicated things. So even though the shortest and fastest route to Ms. Crawley's office would've been across the main playground and through the cafeteria, Tim and Tito agreed to circle the building in the opposite direction and try to get in from the outside. It would take longer, sure, but that was better than risking an untimely smash.

Help Tim and Tito find a safe route.

Tim and Tito were only halfway there when they heard the principal's voice through an open window.

"Target acquired," said Tim, motioning for Tito to follow him.

The two friends flew into the room and landed behind a giant glass tank. Tim stuck his fly-head out and saw that Ms. Crawley was talking to Mr. Balboa, the PE teacher.

Tim scanned the room. There were two sofas, a giant chest freezer, lots of shelves, and a big round table. He'd never seen this room before, which could only mean one thing:

"It's the teachers' lounge!" he buzzed. "JACKPOT!" The teachers' lounge was off-limits to students, so if there was a place where Ms. Crawley kept her secrets, THIS WAS IT!

"I'm sorry, Ofidio, I can't stay today," said Ms. Crawley. "I'm still working on next week's celebration schedule," she sighed. "It's such a pain to keep these little monsters happy!"

Tim and Tito stared at each other; their fly-eyes as big as saucers. They'd been right! Ms. Crawley had been faking her kindness all this time!

Tim turned his attention back to the principal. They were onto something, but they needed more proof.

"I can't wait to leave this place either," said Mr. Balboa. "And look," he said, showing Ms. Crawley his forearm. "My suit is melting with this heat!"

"You should ask Fangs to look into that," said Ms. Crawley. "It's an order."

"Yes, Commander. I will," replied the PE teacher.

Leaving school? Melting suit? Commander? Tim's head was spinning. Suddenly he detected a flurry of movement out of the corner of his fly-eye. Tito must've noticed it too, because they both turned around at the same time. It was a chinchilla, and it was lunging straight toward them like a hungry lion.

Thanks to their lightning-fast reflexes, Tim and Tito could've easily flown away to safety, but they chose not to. Why? Their furry attacker was about to find out the hard way.

The chinchilla smashed its furry head on the tank's glass pane, and Tim and Tito roared with laughter.

"OH MY! What's this?" asked Ms. Crawley, walking toward the glass tank, and prompting the two friends to stop laughing and take cover.

"Fangs brought them," said Mr. Balboa. "She ordered them for a pet-nursing workshop. Nothing suspicious there, right?" He laughed.

"I shall commend her for such a brilliant idea!" said Ms. Crawley, reaching into the tank and inspecting one of the animals. "OH WOW! These are the plumpest, juiciest rodents I've seen in a while! And this one is so warm. . . . I'll take it!" she announced.

The principal hid the chinchilla in her pocket and walked to the door. Tim had many questions, but they would have to wait till later. Ms. Crawley was about to leave!

CHAPTER 8

A DREADFUL DISCOVERY

Flying out of the teachers' lounge was easy. Following Ms. Crawley through a corridor packed full of insect-hating students, however, proved to be much more difficult.

"WATCH OUT!" shouted Tim, as he and Tito dodged swipe after swipe on their way to the principal's office. Tim's tiny heart was racing, but breathing in, and breathing out, he managed to keep his worries in check. Unfortunately, by the time they made it to the door, it was too late. Ms. Crawley had already locked it.

That would've been a bummer . . . if Tim and Tito hadn't been flies.

"Allí, over the door!" said Tito, pointing to a glass pane over the entrance. "We should be able to see everything from there."

Tito was right: from their vantage point they had a perfect view of what was happening inside the office. And what they saw was . . . highly disturbing.

WHAAAAAAT?!

Tim tried to look away, but his eyes were glued to Ms. Crawley. She was about to have lunch.

Now, in normal circumstances, THAT wouldn't be all that shocking—principals are ordinary people, and ordinary people have lunch all the time. What was happening inside that room, however, was neither normal nor ordinary.

First, because Ms. Crawley had a huge mouth, scaly skin, sharp fangs, and a long slithering tongue, which made her look significantly more nightmarish than usual.

And second, because the thing that the mutant principal was holding inches away from her open mouth was—well, you guessed it—none other than the poor CHINCHILLA!

Tim couldn't move, he couldn't think. He couldn't talk, either! All he could do was stare at the scene unfolding before him. Tito was probably experiencing the same thing, because even though flies have a nearly three-hundred-sixty-degree field of view, neither of them noticed the looming shadow creeping behind them.

Just like that, there was a sparkle, a **SWOOSH!**, and Tim felt the unmistakable change in air pressure that indicated that a heavy object was rapidly approaching him.

It was W, with his sparkly Diamond Boy suit, his head-mounted camera, and his diamond-encrusted flyswatter! The annoying kid had heard that two flies were roaming the school, and true to his superhero pledge, he'd rushed to deal with them. He'd found them over Ms. Crawley's door, and since they were out of reach, he'd climbed onto the vending machine next to the principal's office, and with a swing of his arm . . .

GOTCHA!

Unfortunately for W, flies have superhuman reflexes. So much so that, when in danger, they can see the world around them in slow motion. So in the fraction of a second that passed between Tim snapping out of his trance and the diamond weapon smashing into the glass, Tim managed to figure out what was happening, warn Tito, stick his tongue out at W in defiance, take a last look at Ms. Crawley and the poor chinchilla, rub his left eye, hold in a sneeze, stretch out his wings, and fly out of the way. Flies really do have superpowers!

By the time W realized that he'd missed, Tim and Tito had already buzzed out of a window and were headed toward Oskar. Their prehistoric friend would be blown away by what they'd just discovered.

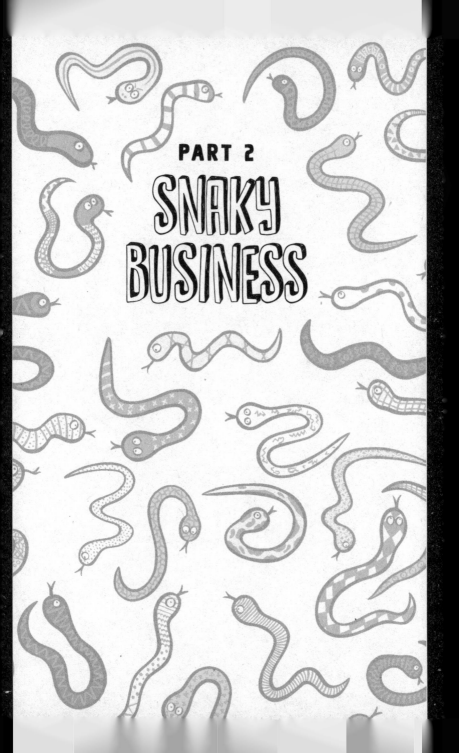

PART 2

SNAKY BUSINESS

CHAPTER 9

OBVIOUS

The conversation with Oskar, though, didn't go the way Tim had imagined.

"Sure, so what?" the dinosaur asked after turning Tim and Tito back to humans. "What's the problem?"

"WHAT DO YOU MEAN, WHAT'S THE PROBLEM?" yelled Tim. "We just told you that the school is run by evil chinchilla-devouring reptilian mutants!"

Oskar shook his head. "First of all, Tim, that's offensive. I believe Ms. Crawley and her friends refer to themselves as Snake People.

"Second, as I already told you earlier, I don't think they're evil. I would know—I once visited a planet packed full of them, and they seemed really nice!

"Third, you should be thanking them for eating those chinchillas! You humans find them cute, but if you could understand what those foulmouthed hairy rats say behind your backs, you'd quickly change your minds.

"And fourth, and most important: Are you telling me that this is the 'big dark secret' that you've been trying to uncover all along? You two didn't know that the teachers were snake aliens?"

Tim couldn't believe what he was hearing. He was shocked, and puzzled, and furious, all at the same time. "OF COURSE WE DIDN'T! ARE YOU KIDDING? HOW COULD WE?"

"Seriously? That's odd," said Oskar, scratching his chin. "It was so OBVIOUS that I thought this was the type of thing that everyone knows but no one talks about. I mean, there were so many clues!"

Like the fact that everything at Leaping Cobra Elementary is connected to snakes: the school's name, the logo, the anthem. . . .

Or the fact that every teacher's name is snake related! Ms. Hiss, Ms. Fangs, Mr. Balboa, Ms. Mamba, Mr. McWriggle, the Spanish teacher—Ms. Ana Conda—and of course the principal, Ms. Crawley. In what world could ALL that be a coincidence?

Tim and Tito stared at each other in silence. Put like that, it did seem pretty obvious indeed.

"Well, now that we've clarified this little misunderstanding, we can move on and find something truly exciting for our next mission," said Oskar.

"Wait, wait! I still think there's something sketchy going on," insisted Tim. "Why would a bunch of reptilian aliens build and run a school on Earth if it weren't for some nefarious purpose?"

"I agree with Tim. Let's talk it over some more later," said Tito. "Now we should head back; the break is almost over."

Tim felt the air leave his lungs. Was it one o'clock already? That was impossible! Unless... Had he lost track of time and completely forgotten about Zoe?

Tim broke into a run without so much as an explanation, and by the time he reached the bleachers, he was panting and covered in sweat.

As for Zoe, she was nowhere to be seen. A chill crept down Tim's spine. This was the second time in as many days that he'd let one of his friends down. And this time he'd messed up even worse. He had promised to bring Zoe lunch. How long had she sat there, tired and hungry, waiting for him? Tim's stomach roared with fury, and his thoughts started to spiral out of control.

Luckily, Tim's impending worries were interrupted by the sounds of hurried steps and police sirens. Confused, he turned around and noticed a crowd gathering by the school's parking lot. A sense of foreboding crept over him. Was it Zoe? *Has something happened to . . . ?* NO! That was a worry he couldn't allow to come true!

Tim took a deep breath, pushed away his mounting headache and his dangerous bubbling worry, and rushed toward the large group of students that had gathered around a TV news van.

CHAPTER 10
BREAKING NEWS

Welcome to MNN. I'm Anderson Scooper, and today I'm live from downtown Metrosalis to give you the scoop of the century! Leaping Cobra Elementary School's principal has been taken into custody by a group of federal agents, minutes after her true identity as a terrifying mutant monster was exposed live on Glitch.

ZUMZUM

That is genius! Now, we still don't know what charges will be brought against her. Can you shed any light on that?

I mean, it's pretty clear that she's a murderous monster. In fact, I'm confident that she was involved in the insect uprising weeks ago.

Now, that's a scoop! And what about the other teachers? We heard that they can't be found anywhere and that they're presumed to be on the run.

Yes, they're all monsters. There's no doubt about it!

That is troubling news! So, as the town's superhero, do you have any comforting message for those in our audience who are now watching TV, scared in their homes?

What I have is a message for the runaway teachers.

I don't know who you really are, and I have no idea what you want. But what I do have is a very particular set of superhero skills that make me a nightmare for beings like you. If you come out and surrender, that will be the end of it. But if you don't, I will look for you, I will find you, and I will make you regret the day you decided to set foot in my town.

You heard it, people! There's no need to fear, because Diamond Boy is on our side!

And now a quick update with some uplifting news! We have just received confirmation that the chinchilla seen in the video is alive and well and is currently receiving psychological attention. Good news, too, for Leaping Cobra Elementary students, as the office of the mayor has just announced that classes have been suspended until further notice, giving hundreds of lucky kids an unexpected vacation in which to enjoy all that our beautiful town has to offer.

CHAPTER 11
BOREDOM

··· MONDAY—<u>ONE WEEK LATER</u> ···

The newscaster couldn't have been more wrong. One week later boredom had taken over Metrosalis, and the school-less students of LCES were feeling downright miserable.

You see, LCES's students had gotten so used to their endless supply of daily awesomeness

and cheerful celebrations that they had become incapable of entertaining themselves. As a result, now that the school and its five fabulous playgrounds were closed, they roamed the town's streets like joyless zombies starving for entertainment.

And you might wonder, weren't there any other places in Metrosalis where kids could go to have a great time? There were! Metrosalis had a fancy cinema, an indoor ice-skating rink, a laser tag arena, and a state-of-the-art VR escape room! The only problem was that every single one of those activities was located inside the giant pyramid-shaped Phara-OH! mall and required the payment of a hefty entrance fee, way beyond the means of ordinary kids' allowances.

And what about other free places? you might ask. Well, unfortunately, the available free options:

(a) Were a bore (like the always-empty
   Metrosalis Museum of the Mustache,
   where Tim's mom worked),
(b) Required putting your life in danger
   (like the Knee-Grater, a hole-infested
   bicycle track by the river), or
(c) Were closed for never-ending
   renovations and widely considered to
   be cursed (like the Metrosalis Park).

To make things worse, the ground beneath the town had started to shake with an ever-increasing frequency, and a growing number of families were forcing their children to spend all day at home.

It was a desperate situation for many, but not for everyone. For the members of Metrosalis's first and only superhero ensemble team, the last seven days had been a flurry of activity.

CHAPTER 12

**DIARY OF A
SPIKY KID**

TOP SECRET

Property of
Tim Sullivan

··· TUESDAY ···

No school. No news from Zoe either. I'm not surprised.
Why should she reach out? I'm the one who bailed on her.
Why do I keep messing things up?

W is ~~a liar~~ the WORST. We've decided to continue our
investigation into the missing ~~teachers~~ Snake People. We
used Oskar's Bignosifier 1.0 to track their scent. We followed
it all the way to the park, but we lost the trail there. The
park is still closed for renovations, but we got in through
the secret entrance that Zoe showed me last Sunday. I
was dreading? hoping? to bump into her there, but no luck
with that, either. I know. I should call her and apologize.
Tomorrow?

··· WEDNESDAY ···

According to the news, Ms. Crawley has been transferred to a high-security prison somewhere out of state. We asked around, but no one has any leads on the missing ~~teachers~~ snakes. We walked Puckles to the park, and Tito used Oskar's Foodifier 3.0 to turn himself into a giant nut to prank a bunch of squirrels. They were terrified. It was fun, and it almost took my mind off Zoe.

I called her twice after coming back home. She didn't pick up, so I left a message asking her to call me. Did I make things worse by waiting too long to apologize? Is she avoiding me? I wouldn't blame her.

··· THURSDAY ···

TODAY THERE WAS AN EARTHQUAKE! It was small and everyone is okay. It took me by surprise, and I almost let a worry slip through. PHEW! We continued looking for the Snake People, but we didn't have any luck. Since we always end up in the park, we've decided to make it the official meeting place of the Justice Three.

Tito keeps asking me about Zoe and keeps telling me that I should ask her to hang out with us. I wish I could tell him the truth about what's happened. He might know what to do. But I can't. She hasn't called back, and she doesn't answer my calls, either. I think the message is clear: she hates my guts.

··· FRIDAY ···

Today I woke up with a terrible headache. I called Zoe again, one last time, just to be sure. Same result.

I was planning to stay home, but Tito heard that someone looking like Mr. Balboa had been seen around the Knee-Grater, so we had to go there to check it out. We didn't find anything, but the place seems to have more holes than the last time I went. There was another small earthquake while we were there! We ended up playing Moon Invaders with Oskar's zero-gravity shoes. We had a good time. I'm glad that Tito and Oskar are still my friends. I'm trying my best not to mess things up with them, too.

··· SATURDAY ···

Today there were two more earthquakes! According to the news, it's some normal ground stuff and we shouldn't worry. Also, a police officer on TV said that the Snake People may have already left the country (or maybe the planet?). Is it time to find another superhero quest? I could use the distraction.

I was still feeling a bit down today, and my stomach was acting weird, but then Oskar took us to see Margot! Guess what? She still remembers the tricks I taught her! She works for a delivery company now. I can tell that she loves it!

··· SUNDAY ···

I wish I could have done things differently. . . . But let's face it, Zoe my friend? It was too good to be true to start with.

There were more earthquakes today. Is it me, or are they getting stronger? Tito says that his neighbor's car disappeared last night. Is there a thief in town?

··· MONDAY ···

It's been a week since the school closed . . . and since I last saw Zoe. I miss talking to her. I wonder how she's doing.

We've decided to stop looking for the Snake People, but we may have a new mission. Stuff keeps disappearing all over town, and it's not only cars but also completely random stuff, like mailboxes and traffic lights. Tomorrow morning we'll meet in the park to discuss ideas to catch the thief.

BAIT?

Detective robot?

CHAPTER 13

THE ENCOUNTER

··· TUESDAY ···

"WE'VE BEEN ROBBED!" yelled Tito, pointing at the spot where their official meeting bench had stood just a few hours earlier. The bench was gone, and so was the willow right next to it.

Tim bent down to inspect the empty space. He frowned. How could a stone bench and a big tree disappear without leaving a trace? It didn't make any sense. "This looks more like the work of a magician than a thief!"

**BARF!
BARF!
BARF!**

Tim perked up at the sound of Puckles, who was barking at a bush.

"What's up, Puckles?" he asked. "Did you find a squirrel hiding in there?"

Puckles continued his incessant barking, so Tim decided to take a closer look. Tito followed him.

"Do either of you recall seeing these holes yesterday?" asked Oskar, who had stayed back, staring at the ground. "I think they might be connected to the disappearance."

"Nah, those are just standard earthquake holes," said Tito, unwrapping his daily bocadillo as he walked. "I've seen them all over town. Unless . . . Are you suggesting that the holes swallowed up a whole tree and our bench?" he asked, then roared with laughter.

"Shh!" Tim shushed his friend, and slowly backed away from the bush. His skin was pale like a ghost's pajamas, and his legs trembled with fright. "They've been swallowed," he whispered. "But not by the holes!" He pointed a trembling finger forward.

There, hunched down behind the bush, sat the creepiest creature that Tim had ever seen. Its back was almost hairless, with pink, wrinkly skin that jiggled as it munched on the last remains of the stone bench.

CRUNCH CRUNCH CRUNCH

When Tito leaned in to take a closer look, Tim stopped him. "It looks dangerous," he whispered. "We'd better leave before it sees us."

Tito nodded and stopped chewing on his sandwich, but then Oskar popped up and yelled at the top of his lungs:

Tim wanted to strangle Oskar. However, that would have to wait for another time. Right now the only thing he could do was try not to faint as the scariest face in animal history stared right at him. The creature had a single red eye, which twitched over a squashed piggy nose. It had paper-thin lips and two slits instead of ears. But the real horror was its mouth. It was lined with row upon row of razor-sharp teeth that glistened with slime and pulsated in and out as if reaching for their next meal.

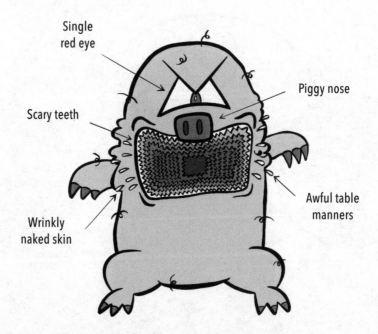

Single red eye

Piggy nose

Scary teeth

Awful table manners

Wrinkly naked skin

"Interesting!" said Oskar, leaning forward. "You're like an even uglier version of a naked mole rat! Do you mind if I take a selfie with you?"

The hideous animal ignored the dinosaur and took a step toward Tim and Tito instead.

Tim's blood froze in his veins. If that thing could chew through rock, he shuddered to imagine what it could do to them. It wasn't a great time to freak out. *Breathe in. Breathe out. Breathe in. Breathe out.*

"¡QUIETO!" yelled Tito, wielding his half-eaten bocadillo as a weapon. "Come any closer, and I'll poke your eye out!"

The beast stopped and let out a long, loud **SCREEEEEECH!** Was it scared? For an instant Tim hoped that Tito's bravery would be enough to keep them safe. But as the ground beneath his feet began to shake, Tim realized that it wouldn't. The creature wasn't afraid of Tito's sandwich—it had called for reinforcements.

CHAPTER 14
DÉJÀ VU

Which brings us back to where we started, with Tim and Tito running for their lives while an army of hungry, sharp-toothed, one-eyed rock-munchers tried to catch them.

Tim peeked over his shoulder. "They're catching up!" he yelled, his heart in his throat.

But just when their chances of survival seemed the bleakest, Tim saw two thick ropes that were hanging from a nearby tree.

"WE'RE SAVED!" Tim cried with joy. "LET'S CLIMB THOSE ROPES!"

His tired legs sped up with a burst of power. They had a chance! Or so he thought. Because do you know those moments, when you think that a situation can't get any worse, and it still does? Well, Tim found out that this was one of those moments, when the two "ropes" suddenly fell from the tree and slithered toward them with their fangs open! Yes. They were giant snakes!

Tim let out a shriek. He and Tito were trapped! Their options were to become either snake snacks or the main dish in a mutant-mole-rat meal. It was an impossible choice! Tim's head was spinning, his stomach was hurting, and the trick about breathing deeply and slowly wasn't working anymore. Things were horrible, but if he let a worry out, they could get even worse. So Tim threw himself onto the ground, covered his head, closed his eyes, and hoped for the best.

And guess what? It worked!

There were screeches, and thuds, and growls, and snaps, and then . . . there was silence. Tim opened his eyes a slit, and seeing no immediate danger, he stood up. He scanned his body, checking that it was all there: two hands, two feet, two ears, one spiky head. . . . *Yes, I'm still in one piece,* he thought, and breathed with relief. And so was Tito, who was standing right next to him with his mouth wide open. What was he looking at?

Tim followed Tito's gaze and discovered the reason for his miraculous survival and for his friend's awed expression. It was the snakes. They

were lying on the ground a couple dozen feet away, their bodies inflated like balloons. They had swallowed the moles whole!

"They're awesome!" said Tito, breaking his silence. "They've saved us!"

Tim was thankful too, really, but there was also the possibility that the snakes might still be hungry. "Let's go!" he whispered to his friend. "We'd better let them digest their food in peace."

Unfortunately for Tim, that was easier said than done, because by the time he turned back around, four giant snakes were already blocking his path. One of the snakes slid forward. Tim gulped. With the moles gone, he and Tito were the only dishes left on the menu. Tim was wondering whether he could convince the snake that he tasted like rotten fish, when a familiar figure waltzed into the scene.

"Oh! There you are!" said Oskar, who was carrying Puckles in his arms. "See, little guy? They're both perfectly safe!"

Perfectly safe, seriously? yelled Tim in his mind. *Don't just stand there. Help us!* He shook his head repeatedly in the snake's direction.

Oskar finally took the hint and noticed the giant reptiles. "Oh, and you found them too!" he said, moving closer. "Good to see you, Mr. Balboa. Long time no see!"

"Mr. Balboa?" Tim mumbled as he lifted his head and stared into the giant reptile's eyes. . . .

The snake smiled. "Oh, there's no need to be so formal anymore. Please call me Ofidio."

Tim's gaze jumped from one snake to another. They were all there, the infamous Leaping Cobra Elementary runaway teachers in their true reptilian forms. Tim and his friends had found them at last. And now . . . What? There was no way they could bring those snakes to justice,

was there? Judging from how easily the snakes had dealt with the mole rats, it was clear that he, Tito, and Oskar were outmatched!

"Please don't tell anyone that you saw us," said a bright-red-skinned snake with a huge belly. Tim recognized her voice immediately; it belonged to their fourth-grade teacher, Ms. Hiss. "It's important that we stay here," she continued. "You must trust us!"

"I don't know, I'm kinda torn," said Tito, rubbing his chin. "On the one hand, you guys just saved our lives. On the other hand, though, you've been lying to us for years and you're wanted criminals. Don't you think that asking us to trust you is a bit much?"

Ofidio nodded. "You're right, we've kept many secrets hidden from you. But now that you've seen firsthand what weremoles can do, perhaps it's time that you learn the truth."

Ofidio took a big breath and began his tale.

CHAPTER 15

THE UNBELIEVABLE TRUE STORY OF THE SNAKE PEOPLE

Everything started on planet Cobra, the third planet in the Great Ophidian system, right at the edge of the Milky Way. There our ancestors lived happy lives, preying upon many rodent species: the giant whale rat, the bouncy mousaroo, the egg-laying chickamole. . . .

No matter how much they ate, their supply of food was limitless, and it was all thanks to the rarest, most powerful element in the universe: the IMPOSSIBLE SOUP™. Our ancestors thought that they'd gathered enough of the precious material to secure our civilization's future forever. However, one fateful day about sixty-five million years ago, they discovered in shock that their entire supply of IMPOSSIBLE SOUP™ was gone.

The effects were immediate: the species they'd been hunting for millennia began to disappear one after another, and soon there was not a single rodent left to eat. Faced with imminent extinction, a small group of people gathered as many supplies as they could find and boarded a spaceship with one clear goal: to travel across the galaxy and find a place with rodent life in which to start over.

Over millions of years, generations upon generation of our people scoured hundreds of thousands of planets, moons, and aster-oids with no luck. But then, fifteen years ago, everything changed. Under the leadership of the young Commander Crawley, we entered your solar system's outer ring and came across a dark world teeming with rodent life. You humans call it Pluto.

We were thrilled! The rodents on Pluto were ugly, and they could eat through anything, but they tasted delicious! We called them the weremoles, and for a while we thought that our problems were over. That is, until we realized something very odd: the planet was shrinking . . . really fast!

We sent a team to investigate underground, and we made a terrifying discovery: the weremoles had a queen, and she was feasting on Pluto from within!

We lost many friends trying to stop that creature. We tried to blast it, to burn it, to zap it, to freeze it. . . . Nothing worked. At last Commander Crawley figured it out. There was only one way to stop that monster and its minions. We had to eat them all!

We succeeded, but the cost of our victory was way too high, and only seven of us ever recovered from that feast.

So with no rodents left on Pluto, and the survival of our species resting on our backs, the seven of us boarded our spaceship and resumed our journey. We were determined to find another planet with less dangerous rodents, but we were so tired and so understaffed that we didn't notice the eighth passenger roaming our ship . . . until it was too late.

By the time we realized that there was a new weremole queen roaming our ship, our supplies were gone, our main engine had been half-chewed, and we were in free fall toward planet Earth.

Our spaceship crash-landed into the lake in this park. We survived, but so did the queen, and in no time she burrowed underground. With only seven of us left and our spaceship damaged and underwater, we knew that we were doomed, and so was this planet.

CHAPTER 16
DOOMED

"Wait a minute there," interrupted Tito.
"That doesn't add up! If you brought a were-mole queen to Earth fifteen years ago, shouldn't our planet have been eaten by now?"

"It should," admitted Ofidio. "However, something incredible happened! When we followed the queen's trail through the tunnels she'd dug underneath this town, we found her inside a massive underground chamber, fast ASLEEP!"

"We had NEVER heard of weremole queens getting tired, so we decided to investigate," continued the snake. "That's when we realized that the queen had fallen asleep directly underneath a traveling circus that was in town that week."

"Wow, that must've been one boring circus performance!" joked Oskar.

The snake ignored Oskar's comment and continued the story. "When the circus left and the queen started to wake up again, we knew that there was a connection. The queen had a weakness, and our only chance of survival was figuring out what it was.

"We tried bringing
in a clown, but it wasn't
the clown.

"We tried bringing in a
lion, but it wasn't the lion.

"We tried bringing
in a juggler, but it wasn't
the juggler.

"We tried bringing in
a fire-eater, but it wasn't
that, either."

"And just when we were about to give up, we figured it out. The queen's weakness wasn't the circus; it was the kids! The sound of human kids' cheers and laughter was so unbearable for the weremole queen that she had to hibernate to block it."

Tim finally understood. "I get it now! With the circus gone, you had to find a new way to keep kids laughing and playing in that area, and there's only one place where you could keep a bunch of kids without raising any suspicions: A SCHOOL! That's why you created LCES!"

"Exactly!" said Ofidio. "But human schools are rarely happy places, so the only way to ensure our survival was to put on human costumes and run the place ourselves." The snake sighed. "With only seven of us, it's not been easy. We've all spent the last fifteen years overworked, each juggling multiple roles in order to make a bunch of human kids happy."

"That sounds rough!" said Oskar. "Why didn't you try to repair your spaceship and leave?"

Tim gave the dinosaur a disapproving frown.

"We fixed our spaceship long ago," explained Ofidio. "Unfortunately, our commander felt responsible for bringing the queen to this planet. She didn't think it was right for us to leave and let you humans fend for yourselves."

"YES, SHE'S A HERO!" yelled a different snake, which Tim recognized as Ms. Mamba. "And look how you humans repay her kindness!"

Tim felt ashamed. Ms. Crawley wasn't the

monster he'd always thought she was.

"Also, we had a plan," continued Ofidio. "We noticed that the more the kids cheered and laughed, the smaller the queen became, so all we had to do was keep the school running until she got small enough for the seven of us to handle her on our own. We were getting really close, but then that annoying video came out and messed it all up! Now, with the commander in jail and the school closed, the queen has finally woken up."

As if on cue, the ground rumbled, louder than ever before. "To make things worse, that monster has started to reproduce, and since her minions' ears are much smaller, those were-moles are immune to her weakness," said the snake. "We've been trying to keep her offspring in check, but we'll be overloaded soon, and when that happens . . . You kids should go back home and try to enjoy whatever time is left. . . . The clock is ticking. This planet is doomed."

CHAPTER 17

THE ALLIANCE

"NO, IT AIN'T!" yelled Tito. "We're not going to let that one-eyed freak destroy our home. It's time for the Justice Three to kick some giant rat's butt!"

Tito's confidence was infectious, but Tim wasn't looking forward to a full-blown confrontation with an army of weremoles. The idea of the world

ending, though, was way less appealing. They had to do something, that was clear, but what?

"Why don't we convince the mayor to reopen the school?" he suggested. "That shouldn't be too hard with Oskar's help!"

"And leave that rat down there?" asked Oskar. "Yuck! No thanks! No rodent is going to try to eat my planet and live to tell the tale. That thing has to go, and I've just come up with the perfect way to do it!"

But before Oskar could explain himself, a pale yellow snake interrupted him.

"Please stop! I know that your intentions are good, but this isn't a game. We're facing a real crisis, with real danger, and there's nothing that a bunch of human kids playing superhero can do to help!"

Tito grinned. "Well, about that . . . Perhaps it's time to show you that you weren't the only ones keeping secrets."

The snakes looked at each other, confused. "What do you mean?" Ofidio asked.

The instant Oskar produced a small remote, Tim knew what was going to happen next: the Snake People were about to have the shock of their lives. The dinosaur pressed a button, a bright glow surrounded them all, and **ZAP!**

The six snakes, the two kids, the dinosaur, and the half-pug, half-pickle hybrid vanished into thin air and reappeared in the center of Oskar's massive entrance hall.

"Welcome to my humble home!" said Oskar.
"Now, shall we begin?"

The looks on the snakes' faces! Tim fought
to hold back a giggle. Their bulging eyes, their
mouths wide open in complete disbelief, their
heads turning left and right, looking for an explanation . . . Yup, he knew the feeling well, but this
was the first time he'd seen others go through
the same thing. This was way more fun.

After Oskar gave a brief explanation of who he was and where (or when) he came from, the three friends gave the six surprised snakes a full tour of the facilities. They were VERY impressed.

"We've seen enough," said Ms. Hiss, while her companions nodded approvingly. "It's clear to us now that the three of you are our best shot at saving the world. Would you help us, please?" The snake extended the tip of her tail in Oskar's direction. Oskar did the same. And so, with a tail shake, the Snake People and the Justice Three agreed to join forces, and at eleven a.m. on that Tuesday morning a historic interplanetary alliance was formed.

"So, what's the plan?" asked Tito.

Tim frowned. *Here it comes.*

"Relax, Tim. You're gonna love it," said Oskar, smiling. "We're going to destroy the weremole queen . . ."

by throwing the biggest party in history!

PART 3
TIME TO PARTY!

CHAPTER 18
THE PLAN

Oskar's plan was simple. They would defeat the weremole queen with the thing she hated the most: kids' cheers and laughter.

"It's pretty easy, really. All we need is a

big venue, a few thousand kids, and to put together the biggest, most amazing party ever in less than twenty-four hours. Then we'll record everyone having the time of their lives and blast that sound on hundreds of loudspeakers that we'll set up as close to the weremole queen as possible.

If everything goes well, the queen should shrink fast, giving you," he said, pointing at the Snake People, "the perfect chance to gobble her up. And voilà, problem solved! Any questions?"

To Tim's surprise, the plan seemed reason-ably safe and kind of made sense! There could only be two explanations for that:

OPTION A:

Oskar was finally learning to keep his wackiness in check. Odds: Not likely.

OPTION B:

Tim had gotten so used to Oskar's wackiness that nothing surprised him anymore. Odds: Yes, this was probably it!

Either way, there was a clear problem, and Tim wasn't the only one to spot it.

"How are we going to make all that happen in just one day?" Ofidio asked.

"Leave the party to us," said Oskar. "You'll be in charge of setting up the loudspeakers and keeping the smaller weremoles in check."

"Actually, that might be a problem," said Ms.

Hiss, patting her bloated belly with her tail. "We won't be able to eat weremoles for much longer. We're already quite full!"

"If only Commander Crawley were here to help!" cried Ms. Mamba. "Her appetite is legendary!"

"It's true, but there's nothing we can do about that," said Ofidio. "We'll have to manage without her. She's also counting on us!" Then the snake turned toward Oskar and added, "There's no time to waste. The main entrance to the queen's burrow is hidden in Metrosalis Park. Can you take us back there, please?"

Tim and Tito stayed behind while Oskar teleported the snakes. It should've taken him just a few seconds, so when five minutes passed and he still hadn't returned, Tim's stomach started to flutter. Had Oskar encountered any trouble? *No, it's Oskar we're talking about. He should be okay,* Tim reasoned. *He'll be here any minute. Focus on your breath. Breathe in. Breathe out. Breathe in. . . .* Ten minutes later, when Tim was about to lose it, Oskar finally reappeared.

And no, he wasn't injured or bruised after an unforeseen battle that could explain his delay. On the contrary, Oskar wore sunglasses, a backpack, and a Hawaiian shirt, and he sipped on a drink in a coconut shell. He looked as cool as a freshly picked cucumber.

"WHAT ON EARTH HAVE YOU BEEN DOING?" yelled Tim, his face red with rage. "Do you think this is the right time for a tropical getaway? We have a party to plan and no time to waste!"

"Calm down. You should relax!" said Oskar. "I was on a tropical island, but not on vacation! I was getting ready for our first stop. Should we get going or what?"

Tim and Tito wrinkled their noses in confusion. "Going? WHERE?!" they asked.

Oskar smiled. "Where else? To rescue Ms. Crawley, of course. Didn't you hear the snakes? We need as much help as we can get!"

Tim was puzzled. "How are we going to rescue Ms. Crawley if we don't even know where she's being held?"

"Tim's right," said Tito. "We've heard that she's been locked in some high-security prison out of state, but that isn't much to go on!"

"Oh, but it is," said Oskar. "You humans are very predictable, and an alien captured by your government can only be in one place." The dinosaur pressed the button on his remote control and . . .

CHAPTER 19

Tim looked around, trying to get his bearings. The three friends had appeared in the middle of nowhere, and besides dust and the occasional cactus, the only thing that he could see for miles was the tall gray concrete wall standing in front of them. There was only one way in, a single metallic door with a big red-and-white sign that read:

Tim gasped.

"QUÉ CHULO!" said Tito, doing his trademark happy dance. "I've always dreamed of visiting a secret military base!"

Tim didn't share Tito's excitement. "No way! Please don't tell me that you want us to get inside there," he said, his palms already sweating. "Haven't you read that sign? They must have a ridiculously high level of security!"

"Sure," said Oskar, placing his backpack on the ground. "Luckily, I have a ridiculously awesome breakout plan."

Tim sighed. He knew that no matter what he said, Tito and Oskar were still going in. Therefore, he had two options: He could refuse to join them and risk being seen as a coward party pooper. Or he could join his friends—*breathe in*—and always be remembered as a good team player—*breathe out*. The choice was clear, even if he didn't like it one bit. "Okay. What's the plan?"

Oskar reached into his backpack. "Glad you asked . . ."

STEP 1: DONUTS

STEP 2: DISTRACT THE GUARDS

At eleven thirty-two hours a timer will go off and launch a giant banana right over the wall.

A giant banana? That won't be enough to distract the guards!

The banana is not for the guards. It's for them, the hungry monkeys! The same timer will open this cage, and our hairy friends will do the rest.

Mayday, Mayday, we need reinforcements! The monkeys have risen, sir. It's happening, it's the Planet of the Apes!

STEP 3: LOCATE THE TARGET

With all the guards busy dealing with the hungry monkeys, we'll roll toward the containment area and locate Ms. Crawley. We should have found her by eleven thirty-five hours.

STEP 4: RELEASE THE PRISONER

STEP 5: PLANT THE DECOY

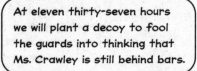

At eleven thirty-seven hours we will plant a decoy to fool the guards into thinking that Ms. Crawley is still behind bars.

Is that an inflatable pool noodle with googly eyes?

Yes, quite a resemblance, right? It will take the army weeks to notice the switch!

Come on, keep blowing!

STEP 6: BEAM OUT

The rescue operation had been a huge success, but Tim, Tito, and Oskar didn't have time to waste on celebrations. The future of the world was at stake, so Oskar beamed them back into his lair, and they set to work. They had less than twenty-three hours to organize the biggest party in history.

CHAPTER 20

MONEY, MONEY, MONEY

"Let's write a list with the things we need to get for the party," suggested Tim, grabbing pen and paper.

"Great thinking, Tim. First of all, we need a venue," said Oskar. "It should be big, popular, and close enough to Metrosalis Park for the loudspeakers to receive the party signal at maximum strength. Any suggestions?"

Tim couldn't think of any venue they could realistically afford. Tito and Oskar, however, weren't concerned about their budget AT ALL.

"What about the Phara-OH! mall?" suggested Tito. "It has a cinema, an indoor ice-skating rink, a laser tag arena, and a VR escape room. It's really cool!"

"That sounds perfect!" said Oskar. "Okay, Tim, write it down. We have to rent the Phara-OH! mall."

Tim tried to object. They didn't have enough money to buy movie tickets, let alone to rent the entire Phara-OH! mall! But before he could say anything, Oskar continued.

"Now, a cinema, an indoor ice-skating rink, a laser tag arena, and a VR escape room are a good start, but that's not nearly enough for the greatest party in history. Tim, please write that we'll also need . . ."

fifty thousand balloons, six hundred bags of confetti, five hundred pounds of assorted candy and snacks (don't forget to add some pickles!), three to four hundred gallons of soda and juice, a cupcake mountain, six bouncy castles, an indoor kart-racing track, a three-thousand-foot-long zip line, an ice-cream-skating rink with a hot-chocolate waterfall, three hundred gaming consoles with all the most popular video games, a pool filled with Jell-O with a minimum of three slides, a cotton candy forest, five smoke guns, three snow cannons, two hundred inflatable sumo suits, a sixty-foot piñata, one thousand piñata-buster sticks, a mechanical bull, a karaoke machine, six hundred water guns, a snowball fighting arena, a five-thousand-square-foot sandbox with its own life-sized sand castle, a build-your-own-giant-teddy-bear workshop, a free surprise-egg dispenser, and a goat!

A GOAT?!

Sure, you never know when you might need a goat! Did you get all that, Tim?

Tim stared at Oskar in silence with his arms crossed.

"What?" asked the dinosaur. "Did I miss anything?"

"Not at all, your list is great," said Tim, with more than a hint of sarcasm. "Or it would be . . . IF WE WERE ZILLIONAIRES! Do you have any idea how much those things cost? We can't afford them!" Seriously, was he the only one there capable of using common sense?

"Money, money, money . . . ," repeated Oskar, shaking his head. "That's all you humans care about!"

The *T. rex* fumbled in his backpack and revealed a crumpled single dollar bill. "There you go!" he said, handing it to Tim. "I was keeping it for an emergency, but I guess this is the right time to spend it. Are we okay now?"

Tim looked at the dollar bill, and then back at his prehistoric friend. Oskar was the smartest being in the universe. However, in matters of money, he was as clueless as a pair of socks at a pool party.

"One dollar? Are you kidding me? This won't even get us a cupcake!" protested Tim. "We'd need millions of these to pay for all the things you mentioned. And I don't know about you two, but I don't have that kind of money lying around!"

"Unfortunately, me neither," said Tito, pulling his empty pockets inside out.

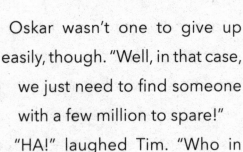

Oskar wasn't one to give up easily, though. "Well, in that case, we just need to find someone with a few million to spare!"

"HA!" laughed Tim. "Who in their right mind would spend that kind of cash on throwing a party for a bunch of kids?"

"We could ask W," suggested Tito. "He has more money than he knows what to do with, and he's always looking for a chance to show it off."

Tim felt the hairs on the back of his neck stand up. "NO. NO WAY! NOT HIM! We're not asking that slimeball for anything!" he yelled, shaking his head. "And even if we could somehow convince him that we're trying to save the world, do you think he'd help us? NOT A CHANCE! The only one W cares about is HIMSELF."

"Perfect!" said Oskar, standing up. "Let's go meet him and offer him exactly what he wants."

CHAPTER 21
THE DIAMONDITES

Tim had never been to W's home. However, everyone in Metrosalis knew where to find it. It was pretty much impossible to miss the massive nineteenth-century palace perched atop Mount Richester. Tim, Tito, and Oskar approached the mansion's gilded gate and rang the bell.

They were greeted by the assistant doorman,

who transferred them to the executive doorman, who in turn referred them to the head
doorman. Yes, W's family employed three
different people to open and close the door.
But wait, there was more, because the head
doorman arranged for them to meet with the
security team, who, after searching and inter-
rogating them for a good ten minutes, allowed
them to speak with a footman, who then

called the underbutler, who introduced them to Alfred, the butler, who finally brought them to the west wing's library antechamber, where they waited patiently for W to appear. And at this point, you might be wondering: How in the world did Tim, Tito, and Oskar manage to convince so many different members of W's household that they were worthy of visiting the young master without an appointment?

The answer is simple. Like this:

"Welcome, welcome," said W, greeting his visitors. "Look at that. I love your costumes! This is such a great surprise. I wasn't aware that I had a fan club already!"

"Oh my gosh, it's him!" said Tito, shaking his hands in the air while jumping up and down like an overexcited fan meeting his idol in person for the first time.

Tim rolled his eyes. Tito deserved an Academy Award for his performance.

"I can't believe we're finally meeting you," said Oskar, shaking W's hand. "We are the Diamondites, the co-founders of the Diamond Boy Forever Fan Club, and we've had an idea that we'd love to run by you."

"Of course, of course," W laughed. "I'm listening."

"Well, as you probably already know, each year the MMAA (the Mutant, Meta-Human, and All-Things-Mighty Association) names a Superhero of the Year, who then gets featured on the cover of their prestigious magazine. It's the ultimate recognition for a superhero, and we, the members of

your official fan club, believe that this year no one deserves that honor more than you."

W beamed with pride. "Oh please, I just do my duty," he said, clearing his throat. "But now that you mention it, YES! I definitely deserve that recognition more than anyone else!"

"That's why we came to see you," added Oskar. "The MMAA will announce their decision soon, and we'd like to ask for your permission to host a party in your honor tomorrow morning. We want to show everyone that you have a lot of support."

"That's brilliant!" said W, jumping out of his seat. "I'm definitely in! Where are you going to host it?"

Oskar sighed. "The only thing we can afford to rent is a small garage downtown. It's a pity, because you deserve better! But don't worry, one day we'll be able to put together a party in your honor as flashy and as big as the ones hosted by the fan clubs of the Amazing Bulk or

Ratwoman. For the time being, though, that's way out of our league."

"NO, IT ISN'T!" yelled W. "Alfred, where are you? Quick, bring me my credit card!" he ordered.

W placed the shiny card into Oskar's hands. "Take this. Spend whatever you need. I don't care how much it costs. Just make sure that you put together the biggest, most successful party in history. Will you do that for me, please?"

Tim, Tito, and Oskar smiled at each other. "Well, if you insist . . ."

CHAPTER 22
THE INFLUENCER

With enough money to buy a country (if they wanted to), it didn't take long for the three friends to set up everything they needed for the big event. There was only one thing left to do. All their efforts would be for nothing if they couldn't get enough kids to attend the party. Unfortunately, that was proving harder than they'd thought.

"I've hired the DJ and the marching band of penguins already," said Tim, twisting to stretch his back. "That should take care of the music. How are the RSVPs looking?"

"Not great," said Tito. "It's been hours since W announced the event on Glitch, and we still have less than one hundred confirmed guests."

Tim groaned and turned toward Oskar. "See? I told you that turning this party into a Diamond Boy celebration was a terrible idea. Not even the people who think W's a hero want to come!"

"What if I built a child magnet powerful enough to pull every kid in a hundred-mile radius toward us?" suggested the dinosaur. "That would solve our problem in no time!"

"Are you kidding? That's called KIDNAPPING!" Tim snapped. "And we need kids to cheer, not to cry for their mommies!"

"That's fine!" said Oskar. "I bet I could get them laughing in no time with a few of my jokes."

Tim reached out for his cup of water. He wasn't even going to bother commenting.

"What we really need is an influencer," said Tito.

"An influenza? How is that going to help?" asked Oskar. "If everyone has the flu, no one will be able to join the party!"

Tito giggled. "Not the influenza. AN INFLUENCER!" he repeated. "Someone famous, with many followers on social media ready to do whatever that person does."

"I see. That makes more sense," admitted Oskar. "And do you happen to know anyone like that?" he asked.

Tito's smile widened. "Not only do I know her, but I've already asked for her help. She's

super popular, she has thousands of followers on Instaglam, and she just happens to be a
good friend of Tim's."

WHAT? Tim almost poured the water all over
himself. *Tito must be kidding, right?* He couldn't
mean . . . **DING-DONG!** The doorbell rang.

"Tim, please go open the door," said Tito.
"That must be Zoe!"

PBBBBT! Tim spat water all over the table.

CHAPTER 23

TRUST

Tim approached the front door, his heart about to gallop out of his chest. Was Zoe really standing on the other side? This could be the second opportunity that he'd been wishing for all week; he couldn't let it go to waste! And so, with a deep breath, he reached out for the door-knob and opened the door.

Tim and Zoe stood in silence for a second. "Wait, YOU'RE sorry?" they both asked, pointing at each other.

The hint of a smile formed at the corner of Zoe's mouth.

"JINX!" the two kids shouted together before bursting into laughter.

"I'm sorry I didn't call you back," said Zoe once the laughter had died down. "I've been out of town since last Monday, and I didn't have my phone with me. My father is seriously scared of snakes, and he freaked out so much when he saw the video of Ms. Crawley on the news that he packed our bags in a rush and drove us across the country. We stayed a few days with my grandpas while things calmed down, and we just returned."

"No, I'm the one who should apologize!" said Tim. "I told you that I'd have lunch with you last Monday and I didn't show up. I tried, but I was . . . in the middle of something. Ugh. I know it's not a great excuse, but I'm really, REALLY sorry."

"It's all good!" said Zoe, wiping the whole issue away with a wave of her hand. "I knew that something urgent must've come up. I was worried about you, actually, but I was relieved when I saw you in the crowd as we were driving away from school."

Tim felt his muscles relax, as if a great weight had been lifted off his chest. His persistent headache, the nagging discomfort in his belly, they were suddenly gone. He smiled, and if Zoe hadn't been right there, watching, he might've even done a happy dance.

"So, Tito told me that you needed my help," said Zoe. "What can I do for you?"

Tim took a moment to consider how much to tell her. This would be a perfect chance to come clean and tell Zoe everything that was going on, starting with the fact that Oskar was a time-traveling dinosaur, and ending with their plan to stop the giant weremole from eating their planet from the inside. But how would she take it? Would she believe him? *Probably not.* And even if she did, would she run away frightened and decide that she was better off not being his friend?

Tim shuddered. NO. He couldn't take that risk. Not now! So instead he stuck with the basics. "Me, Tito, and Oskar are putting together a party to honor Diamond Boy, and we'd like you to join us, and we'd love it if you could invite your followers on social media, too."

"Wait. YOU are organizing a party for W?" Zoe stared at Tim with such an intense gaze that he feared she'd be able to see right into his head.

Tim recoiled instinctively. "Well, yes, you see . . ."

Zoe shrugged. "It's fine, you don't have to tell me. I'm your friend, Tim, I trust you. And even though I can tell that there's more to this than you're letting on, I'm sure that you have your reasons to keep it secret. I just want you to know that you can trust me, too, okay?"

Tim's cheeks flushed a bright red. He did trust Zoe. . . .

"I'll help you," Zoe said, interrupting Tim's thoughts. "But I'll need something in return."

Tim gulped. "Wh-wh-what?"

It was now Zoe's turn to hesitate. "So . . . the thing is . . . I don't usually go to parties," she said, playing nervously with her hair. "I always feel so awkward at them, as in . . . I don't belong. However, if you're there with me"—Zoe lowered her eyes—"I think it will be fun! So, I know this might sound silly, but . . . can you promise me that you won't leave me alone?"

Tim couldn't believe his ears. Was Zoe, the most popular girl in town, nervous about attending a party? She was so good at everything that he'd never imagined her to have such a vulnerable side. But she did, and she'd shown it to him! "I promise," Tim said with unusual conviction. "We'll stick together, and we'll have an unforgettable time!"

CHAPTER 24
ALMOST THERE

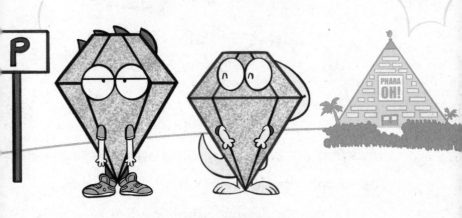

··· WEDNESDAY ···

The big day had arrived, and at ten a.m.
the area surrounding the Phara-OH! mall was
buzzing with thousands upon thousands of kids
waiting for the doors to open. Everything was
going according to our heroes' plan; there was
just one tiny detail to take care of. Tim and Oskar,
dressed in their Diamond Boy Forever Fan Club
costumes, waited in the parking lot for the "guest
of honor" to arrive.

"What are we going to do about W? I can't spend the day following him around dressed like a diamond," Tim complained. "I promised Zoe I'd be with her, and I'd rather be eaten by a weremole than let her see me like this!"

"Relax, all is taken care of." Oskar smiled. "I have a hunch that our shiny friend won't be staying for long."

As if on cue, the sound of a helicopter thundered overhead. Tim looked up. Even from a distance it was easy to tell who it belonged to. How many other people would ride a helicopter fully covered in diamonds?

The chopper landed, and Oskar and Tim—or should we say "the two Diamondites"—moved forward to greet their guest.

"What an impressive turnout!" said W, leaping to the ground in front of them. "You've done a great job! Bravo!"

Tim raised a hand to his eyes; under the morning sun, every single move W made in his Diamond Boy costume sent sparkles in all directions.

Oskar smiled. "Thank you, but the real merit is yours. Everyone is here because of you."

"Hoo, hoo, hoo," W guffawed. "That's so true!"

It wasn't. At least not 100 percent. Even though W's money had paid for the party, and hundreds of posters of his snotty face were plastered all over the place, the person that almost everyone there had come to meet was Zoe, not him. No one had told him that, though. "I've prepared a short two-hour speech to thank my fans," the kid announced. "Should I give it now before we head in?"

Tim glanced at Oskar. "Two hours?" he whispered. "Everyone will leave! What do we do now?"

Oskar remained calm. "You'll find out in three . . . two . . . one . . ."

AIEEE! Tito, in his diamond-shaped costume, broke through the crowd. "HELP! HELP! SOMEBODY HELP!" he yelled.

"What happened?" asked Oskar. "Is anything wrong?"

"AN INSECT! A HORRIBLE INSECT!" Tito wailed. "I'VE JUST SEEN IT!"

Tito should seriously consider a career in acting, thought Tim.

"Don't you worry, my dear fans," said W, speaking more to the gathered audience than to Tito himself. "I, Diamond Boy, your favorite superhero, will take care of that disgusting insect and protect you all!" Then he reached over his shoulder and slowly unsheathed his diamond-encrusted flyswatter. "Now tell me, my friend, where did you see that bug?"

Tito pointed up, and a few hundred kids gasped in unison.

"LOOK, IT'S THERE!"

It was obvious to Tim that W was expecting a normal insect, some poor bug that he could easily whack. He believed he'd score some extra fame points and go on with what he thought would be a day of self-celebration. Unfortunately, he was in for a surprise. Because what Tito was pointing at was no ordinary insect—in the sense that no ordinary insect would be able to land on top of a parked helicopter and crush it under its weight. As you might've already guessed, Tito was pointing at MARGOT!

At the sight of the giant fly, W's legs began to shake, and judging from his terrified expression, he was just about ready to flee. But then Oskar shouted, "This monster is no match for our mighty hero. LET'S HEAR IT FOR DIAMOND BOY!" and the crowd gathered around them started to chant W's name.

At that point W must've realized that he

couldn't back down with so many people watching him. The kid clenched his fists, raised his flyswatter, and let out a scream as he sprinted toward the ten-thousand-pound fly. Margot took off, and so the chase began.

CHAPTER 25

FUN, GAMES, AND A (W)HOLE LOT OF TROUBLE

It was ten thirty a.m. when the doors to the Phara-OH! mall finally opened, and the gathered crowd stormed through the entrance, ready to explore the pyramid's twenty-eight floors of wacky, unrestrained fun.

"Are you ready?" asked Tim, who had managed to change back into his usual clothes before Zoe's arrival.

Zoe pulled him by the arm and charged forward. "Come on, Tim. Let's go."

To say that the following two hours were awesome would be a huge understatement. Tim and Zoe raced karts through a cotton candy forest, teamed up for an epic snowball fight, and rode an absurdly long zip line that landed them in a bouncy pool of Jell-O. Next they went ice-cream-skating, and Tim's balance was so hilariously bad that by the time they finished, he was covered in vanilla ice cream from head to toe.

"Do you want to climb the cupcake mountain on the tenth floor next?" asked Tim.

"Sure, but shouldn't we stop by a restroom first?" giggled Zoe. "You look like a giant sundae!"

Everything was going great, and judging from all the cheers and laughter that Tim could hear around him, it shouldn't take long for the weremole queen to become small enough to be taken care of. So why on earth wasn't he happy? Even right then, as he walked down the corridor laughing alongside Zoe, he couldn't ignore the gnawing feeling that something was off. Had something happened to the Snake People? Was he feeling anxious because Tito and Oskar were once again having fun without him? Or was it something else altogether?

Tim tried the usual techniques to manage his worries, but since he couldn't pinpoint what was bothering him, the feeling was proving hard to control. His head rang with pain, and the pit in his stomach grew larger with every step he took. It was silly. It didn't make any sense! He had no reason whatsoever to

be feeling like that. And yet . . . *WHAT IF I do?*
WHAT IF something has gone horribly wrong?

Tim halted, his face stricken with guilt. The moment the flutter in his stomach eased, he realized what he'd done. He'd turned the impossible into unlikely, the unlikely into plausible, the plausible into possible, the possible into likely, and the likely into certain. He didn't know what, when, or how, but now, without a doubt, he knew that something had gone horribly wrong.

"Are you okay?" asked Zoe, turning around.

Tim hesitated. *What now?* "I have to go find Tito and Oskar," he said, running to the elevator. "Something really bad is about to happen. You should leave!"

Zoe ignored Tim's request and chased after him. "No way! We promised to spend the day together, remember? I don't care what's going on, I'm coming with you!"

The two kids reached the deserted lobby at the same time. Tim leaned over with his hands on his knees. "It's too dangerous," he

said, trying to catch his breath. "You have to believe . . ."

Tim's voice trailed off at the sight of the gaping hole in the floor. He jolted. *OH NO!* A quick scan of the room revealed several other openings, and when Zoe asked, "Can you hear those crunching noises?" Tim's suspicions were confirmed. A hideously wrinkly head emerged from one of the holes. And then another. And then a few more. "Stay behind me. We're in trouble," Tim whispered.

CHAPTER 26

WHACK-A-MOLE!

"What are those things?" Zoe asked. "That one's chewing a trash can!"

"It's a long story," said Tim. "But trust me, they're bad news." He kept his eyes on the incoming weremoles while he looked around for a weapon. Unfortunately, lobbies are not usually equipped with rodent-proof weaponry, so he ended up grabbing the only thing he could find: a WET FLOOR sign made of bright yellow plastic.

Tim brandished the sign at the creatures, but the weremoles didn't flinch; they kept getting closer and closer, their teeth reaching outward in anticipation of their next meal.

"Should we make a run for it?" suggested Zoe.

Tim nodded, trying his best to remain cool. "Let's do it. With any luck they'll follow us outside before anyone else sees them. I know this might sound weird, but the party must go on; that's the most important thing!"

Of course, no sooner had Tim said that than a door opened behind them and a large group of stick-wielding, sugar-rushed kids stormed into the lobby. They'd just finished smashing the giant piñata that Tim, Tito, and Oskar had hung up in the VR escape room, and they'd eaten so much candy that they were bursting with energy. The hyper kids and the hungry weremoles stared at each other. Tim could feel the tension in the air. If chaos erupted, their plan to stop the were-mole queen was doomed!

Or not.

Because without a moment's hesitation, Zoe ran toward a little girl who was holding two whacking sticks twice her size, and asked, "May I have one, please?" The girl nodded timidly and handed Zoe one of the rods. Zoe turned around, stormed toward a weremole that had just popped out of a hole in the floor near her, and gave it such a tremendous WHACK! that the creature disappeared into the hole and was never seen again.

WHACK!

"OH MY GOSH! OH MY GOSH!" yelled the little girl, her eyes as big as saucers. "THERE'RE HOLES . . . THERE'RE MOLES . . . IT'S A GIANT WHACK-A-MOLE GAME!"

After that it was chaos, but the good kind. The battle that ensued will live on in the annals of history as the most entertaining conflict of all time. Word spread fast, and more kids joined in the action, and even though new weremoles kept popping up too, the ugly rock-munching monsters quickly discovered that they were powerless against one of the most destructive forces on the planet: a mob of fearless kids on a sugar high.

Best of all, everyone was having a great time!

"Things here are under control," said Zoe. "What next?"

"That . . . that's all," lied Tim, trying not to look Zoe in the eyes. Thanks to her, the crisis had been averted. However, Tim knew better than to declare an early victory. The fact that were-moles were appearing in the mall was a clear sign that something terrible had happened. Had the Snake People been defeated? Was there a problem with the broadcast? Tim couldn't tell, but the following was certain:

1. Whatever it was, it was his fault, and
2. With the future of the planet at stake, and with Oskar and Tito having fun who-knows-where in the upper twenty-eight levels, it was up to him to make things right. Yes, even if it meant risking his life.

"I . . . I gotta go check something out," said Tim, trying to smile as he hurried toward the exit.

"You stay here." *Safe.* "I . . . I'll be back. Soon!" *Or perhaps not?*

But before Tim could leave, a hand grabbed him by the shoulder. "Not so fast, my friend," said Zoe, with a frown on her face and an unusual edge in her voice. "I might not understand what's going on, but I can tell that you need my help. I'm coming with you!"

All it took was one look into Zoe's determined eyes for Tim to realize that arguing was pointless. "Okay, but . . . it's going to be dangerous!" he warned.

Zoe tapped the whacking stick on her hand and smiled. "I wouldn't hope for anything less."

Tim shrugged. He could certainly use Zoe's help; she'd already proven to be way more capable than him when dealing with the alien rats. "Let's go, then!" he said, opening the glass door for Zoe. "I'll fill you in on the details while we get there. First, though, we need to find a ride."

Tim scanned the empty parking lot, and that was when he saw the goat.

CHAPTER 27

DANCING WITH WEREMOLES

Let's be honest, there are cooler ways for a superhero to make an entrance than riding on a goat's back. But Tim didn't care; he had much bigger issues on his mind, like:

- Not falling and breaking his neck,
- Keeping his mounting worries in check, and most important,
- Pretending not to notice that Zoe was holding tight to his chest.

"We're here," Tim said when they reached the large dish antenna that Oskar had set up in the park, right by the entrance to the queen's burrow. There were giant colorful inflatable balls strewn everywhere—that was weird—but something eerier caught Tim's attention first. "This place is way too quiet," he whispered, barely managing to keep his teeth from chattering.

He had a point. Not far from there, inside the burrow, two hundred speakers should have been blasting the cheers and laughter from the biggest party ever. So why couldn't he and Zoe hear a sound?

Zoe knelt on the ground. "I found the problem," she said. "The wires are all burnt! Isn't that odd?"

Tim had a coughing fit. On their ride there, he'd told Zoe about the weremole queen and the Snake People, but he'd decided against mentioning his unfortunate superpower or his role in creating the current mess. "Yes, super odd," Tim agreed. He cleared his throat. "Any-way, where's everyone?"

Out of nowhere came a cracked, reedy voice: "He . . . re . . ."

Tim looked around, confused, and stumbled upon a face on one of the giant inflatable balls. "M-M-Ms. Crawley?" Tim stuttered. "Is that you? What happened?"

"Too . . . ma . . . ny . . . Too . . . full . . . So . . . rry . . ." The words died down as the bloated snake closed her eyes and fell into a deep slumber.

Tim humphed. He was starting to puzzle out what had happened. *Ms. Crawley and the others must've been overrun by weremoles after my worry burnt the wires and the speakers stopped working.* It was clear what he and Zoe had to do. "We have to get those speakers working again!" he yelled.

"I'm not sure that's possible," said Zoe. "But I've figured out a way to play the broadcast on my phone." She pressed a button on her phone's screen, and suddenly the silence around them was broken by the sound of thousands of kids having a blast. "I'm afraid that's as loud as it goes, though," she said.

Tim felt a glimmer of hope. "That's awesome, Zoe!" he said. "That might be enough to ensure that the queen remains asleep while we get Oskar. He should be able to repair this mess in no time!"

At that same moment a deafening **ROAR**

came from deep within the burrow, shaking both the ground and whatever little confidence Tim had gained. And to make matters worse . . .

"Watch out, Tim, weremoles incoming!"

Tim looked up and saw five familiar one-eyed faces emerge from the burrow's entrance. *Oh NO!*

He took a step back, and then another, and then a third, and then . . . he tripped over the wires! "NOOO!"

The weremoles didn't waste any time, and seeing an opportunity for an easy meal, they rushed to the attack. All Tim could do was stare in horror as five mouths and who-knows-how-many-million teeth rushed to get a piece of him.

"Duck!" Zoe yelled.

Tim lowered his head, and BAM! BAM! BAM! BAM! BAM! the five weremoles met the painful end of Zoe's whacking stick.

"Are you okay?" asked Zoe, offering her hand to help Tim stand up. He looked at his friend in awe. She was an angel. A stick-wielding, alien-rat-smashing angel!

"You're amazing!" he mumbled, a bit too loudly.

Luckily, Zoe didn't seem to have noticed. "It'll take more than that to stop them," she said, her eyes fixed on the weremoles, which were starting to recover from the blows. "I'll handle them. You take this." Zoe handed Tim her cell phone and a small object that he immediately recognized as her earphone case. "Put these on the queen's ears," she instructed. "That will stop her for sure!" And with those words, she sprang into action.

WHACK!

EEK!

AHH!

SWISH!

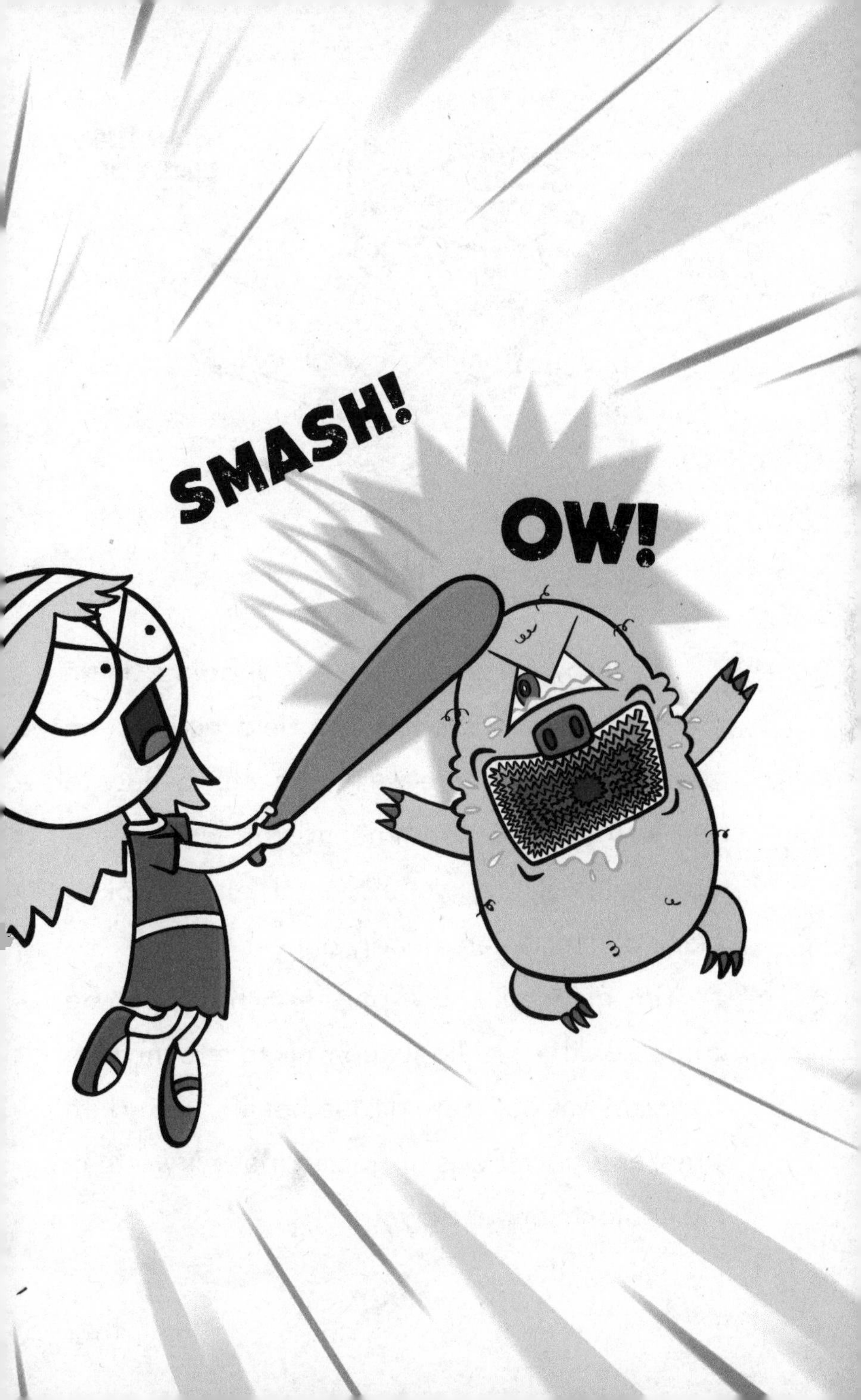
SMASH!
OW!

HOW TIM SEES ZOE.

Tim took a last look at the ongoing battle from the burrow's entrance. He'd never seen anything like it. There was a graceful beauty to the way Zoe was pummeling the weremoles. She was swift, firm, yet also nimble; she looked like a dancer, a very deadly dancer.

Tim glanced at the phone in his hand. He turned on the flashlight and walked into the burrow. Zoe was out there risking her life to buy him time, and now it was his job to make it worth it. He couldn't let her down.

CHAPTER 28

JUST KEEP LAUGHING

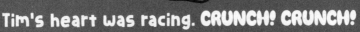

Tim's heart was racing. CRUNCH! CRUNCH! CRUNCH! All around him the tunnel's walls trembled with the sound of hard rock being ground into dust. The noise was so deafening that the cheers and laughter coming out of Zoe's phone were barely noticeable. *WHAT IF it isn't loud enou–?* Tim took a deep breath; he couldn't afford to trigger his worries once again.

The phone would work. It had to! There was no other way.

But when Tim entered a large open space and inadvertently pointed his flashlight straight at the weremole queen's face, his determination fizzled out. The two-hundred-foot-tall monster—which was so terrifying that it made the weremoles outside look like harmless little puppies—let go of the massive boulder it was munching on and dropped down onto all fours. Its single eye scanned the ground ahead until it locked on Tim. The monster roared. **RAAAWWR!**

A storm of slime, spit, and pebbles buffeted Tim with such force that he was blown back over twenty feet. The queen sprang forward, her giant mouth wide open, ready to swallow Tim.

Unable to run or hide, he raised his arm and pointed Zoe's phone toward the incoming rodent. It was his only hope, but the sound coming out of the speaker couldn't be heard over the stomping of the monster's feet on the ground. Tim gasped. This was it; neither Zoe nor Tito nor Oskar was going to save him this time. He flinched, bracing for the worst, and then, out of sheer desperation, he laughed.

HAHAHAHAHA!

The queen ground to a halt inches away from him.

HEEHEEHEE! Tim laughed even harder. The creature shook its head, crying in pain.

WAKAKAKAKA! Tim hollered at the top of his lungs, as if his life depended on it.

The rodent backed down, and after giving Tim a final hateful look, it collapsed on the ground and began to snore. Tears ran down Tim's face. It had worked!

Tim stood up; his limbs were wobbly like pudding. His throat was starting to feel raw from all the forced laughter, but he couldn't risk stopping until the earphones were firmly secured to the queen's ears. He didn't have much time—his voice wouldn't hold forever—so he swallowed hard and approached the slumbering giant.

It was huge. So huge, in fact, that even though the monster was lying down, its ears were still well out of Tim's reach. There was only one way to get to them: he had to climb up the rodent's snoring face. At that realization, a chill went through him, and he almost stopped laughing. *Wouldn't it be nice if my life wasn't always such a mess?*

Tim pocketed Zoe's phone. The queen's body emitted a faint green glow, and now that his eyes had adjusted to the darkness, that was all he needed to find his way around. Next he took Zoe's earphones out of their case and brought them close to his own ear to make sure that they were working properly. They were. *Okay, here goes nothing,* thought Tim. He looked up, swiped the sweat from his forehead, wiped it on his pants, cracked his stiff fingers, and started to climb.

Whoever thinks that being a superhero is a glamorous job has clearly never tried to climb the face of a two-hundred-foot-tall snoring rat by grabbing on to its wrinkly, drool-drenched cheeks. The queen's heavy breathing, combined with skin slipperier than a toad's back, made Tim's climb not only disgusting but also excruciatingly hard and slow. So much so that by the time Tim made it to the monster's snout, he was so out of breath that he was forced to take a break. Suddenly the hairs on his neck stood straight up; something was amiss. At first he couldn't tell what it was; the burrow was in complete silence. But then he realized, in horror, that THAT was precisely the problem: his voice was gone, and even worse, the queen's snoring had completely stopped.

CHAPTER 29

POWER

The weremole queen stirred awake and staggered to her feet. Meanwhile, up on the creature's nose, Tim was clinging on to a thick, long hair for dear life. The monster sniffed the air and roared with rage. Tim gulped. He didn't speak Weremole, but he didn't need a translation dictionary to know that the giant alien rat was looking for him.

It wasn't hard to imagine what would happen if the queen found him, or if he fell down, or even worse, if he wasn't found and didn't fall, and had to spend the rest of his life holding on to a rat's gnarly hair. All the options he could think of were awful, and Tim's belly gurgled as he struggled to shut down the flood of worries rushing to his head. Then things got worse.

"Tim, are you okay?" came Zoe's voice, from somewhere down the tunnel.

HELLO?

The queen crouched low, her single eye fixed on the cavern's entrance. Tim's stomach did a somersault. The monster was readying to attack. Zoe was in grave danger!

He had to do something. Fast! But what? Tim stared at the two earphones that he still held in his hand. The sound was barely audible from that distance, but he could feel the cheers and laughter tickling his skin.

If only the queen could hear them too! Tim mentally measured the distance to the creature's right ear. Even if he caught the monster by surprise, the odds of him making it there were practically nonexistent. But as the echo of Zoe's steps grew closer and closer, and the pressure on Tim's chest continued to grow, he realized that he had no other option. He let go of the hair and broke into a run.

As he sprinted down the edge of the queen's snout, Tim thought of his mom. She'd be really sad to hear that her son had been eaten. He thought of Rachel, his sister, too. They didn't talk much, but she'd surely notice that he was gone. The weremole shook its massive head, and Tim leaped forward. He also thought of Zoe. He should've told her the truth, the entire truth, but now it was too late. Would she ever know that he did trust her?

Tim leaped again, using the rodent's wrinkled skin as a foothold. He finally thought of Tito, and Oskar. They would definitely miss him, wouldn't they? He felt a pang of doubt, and his legs refused to go on. A giant pink paw, with blade-like claws, zoomed toward him, and yet all he could think of was his two friends back in the Phara-OH! mall, having the time of their lives. WHAT IF the reason Tito and Oskar were having so much fun was that he wasn't there with them? Tim's belly fluttered with a strength that he'd never felt before, and out of nowhere, it was almost as if he could really hear his friends, cheering and laughing their hearts out.

The paw stopped midair. *Wait, is this sound real?* Tim's eyes darted to his clenched fist, and for the first time ever, he realized that there was a way to harness his power

FOR GOOD.

Tim raised his arm and pointed the ear-phones forward. He closed his eyes, but this time to better focus on his worry. He welcomed it, letting it feed on all the insecurities and fears that he'd been blocking for so long.

WHAT IF everyone at the party is having a much, MUCH better time now that I'm not around?

The impossible turned into unlikely, the

HA! HA! YAY! HOO! AAH!

unlikely into plausible, the plausible into possible, yada, yada, yada, and as the butter-flies in Tim's stomach grew bigger and louder, so did the sound coming from the earphones.

It got so loud, in fact, that Tim had to let the tiny devices go so that he could cover his own ears. The weremole queen screamed in pain, unable to fall asleep while the entire burrow shook with the cheers and laughter of thousands of kids having an impossibly immense amount of fun. And then . . .

CHAPTER 30

AN AFTERNOON SNACK

"Tim, can you hear me? TIM!"

Tim opened his eyes and found Zoe's face so close to his that for an instant he thought he'd died and gone to heaven. But with one quick look at his surroundings, he remembered where he was. "The queen!" he yelled, springing off the ground. Tim clutched his neck. His voice was raspy, but it had returned. "Where is that monster? What happened?" he asked.

"I'm not sure," said Zoe. "I heard a deafening sound, and then an explosion, and when I got here"—she placed something in Tim's hand—"this is what I found."

It took Tim a second to process what he was looking at. A tiny one-eyed rodent was lying immobile on his palm. Could it be? It had to be! Tim smiled. He'd done it; he'd harnessed the power of his worries! It had worked! And it felt incredible. "Do you think it's dead?" he asked.

"I doubt it," said Zoe. "Look carefully at its chest. It's still moving."

Tim's happiness faded away. If the queen

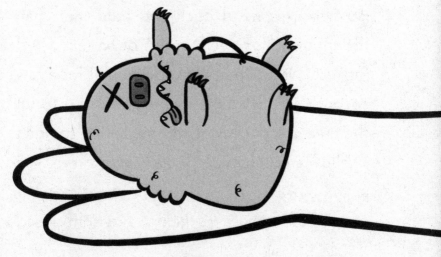

woke up and managed to escape, everything they'd done would be for nothing. "We have to finish the job now that we have the chance," he said. Tim racked his brain, trying to recall what the Snake People had told him about defeating this monster, and when he did, his stomach churned with disgust. "There's only one way to stop the queen," he explained. "I have to eat her!"

"WHAT?" Zoe's cheeks turned white, and she covered her mouth with both hands. Tim felt just as grossed out, but with the Snake People too full to help, there was no other choice. He tilted his head back and held the small rodent over his open mouth. Zoe shrieked and looked away. Tim remained like that for a few seconds. . . . His fingers were refusing to let the creature go! It was too much. He couldn't swallow an alien rat, especially when it was still alive!

You have to do it. It's the only way! Tim closed

his eyes and pinched his nose; that usually worked when he had to take some awful-tasting medicine. But it was useless now. *Come on, Tim, just open your fingers and swallow. Do it for the sake of the world! I bet weremoles taste like chicken.*

Do they? Unfortunately, we'll never know. Because the queen regained consciousness, bit Tim's finger, leaped to the ground, and darted toward the exit.

Tim and Zoe broke into pursuit. "We can't

let her escape!" Tim yelled. Zoe was faster than Tim, but the rodent was even faster than Zoe, and by the time they made it out, the queen was gone.

"Let's split up. She can't be far!" said Zoe.

Zoe went to look around the big dish antenna, so Tim decided to check the area next to the bloated snakes. He heard a rustle, and then he saw her. The rat raced into the bushes, with Tim on its tail. It was escaping once again! Tim looked up in despair and saw an opportunity: the path ahead was blocked by the goat!

Knowing that this was his only chance, Tim didn't hesitate. He threw himself forward with his arms extended, ready for the catch. But yet again the queen slid right through his fingers, and with one quick jump over the goat's back, the rodent leaped toward freedom.

Tim watched, powerless, as the alien rat arched through the air, about to disappear from his sight forever. He couldn't see the monster's ugly face from there, but he could feel it smiling. The queen had won, he had lost, and the world would pay the price.

But just as that thought crossed his mind, a massive shadow zipped through the sky above, and something burst out of the bushes.

It was tall, it was shiny, it was swinging something up and down, and most important, it had an open mouth screaming its lungs out. That is, until it swallowed something accidentally.

GULP!

YEP, it was W. And this time, for once, he'd really saved the world.

PART 4
WRAPPING UP

CHAPTER 31

ENDS . . .

Over the next few weeks, life in Metrosalis slowly went back to normal. The earthquakes, the holes, the disappearing trees, the missing teachers, they were all soon forgotten, but the awesomeness of the party that had taken place on that fateful Wednesday lived on in the memory of an entire generation of kids.

Have I told you the story of how I went to the biggest party ever?

- 70 years later -

Leaping Cobra Elementary remained closed, and since it would take a while to find a new team to run it, the mayor decided to let its students take an early summer vacation.

As for the Snake People, they eventually recovered from their acute case of extreme rodent indigestion, thanks in no small part to Oskar's intensive care.

And then they packed their things, bid farewell to our heroes, and went . . . well, not that far away.

So . . . are you leaving Earth, then?

No way! There're too many yummy rodents on this planet, and we found the perfect cover!

That's all good to know. But what about Tim and his friends? Let's go back in time and see what happened the day after the party.

CHAPTER 32
... AND BEGINNINGS!

··· THURSDAY ···

BAM! BAM! BAM! Tito slammed his gavel on the table. "I declare this meeting of the Justice Three open," he said. "Our first order of business is welcoming our new member, the incredibly talented Zoe Charms!"

Zoe smiled and waved her hand while Tim, Tito, and Oskar clapped enthusiastically.

"Tim told us what you did yesterday," Tito said. "I think he used the word 'amazing' more than twenty times." Tim's ears grew red while Tito chuckled. "I can't wait to fight for justice alongside you!"

"I'm so happy to be part of this!" cried Zoe with excitement. "I was a bit shocked at first," she said, looking at Oskar and at Tim. "But thank you, Tim, for trusting me with the truth!"

The redness on Tim's ears extended to the rest of his face.

"So, should we change our name to the Justice Four, then?" suggested Oskar.

Puckles and Waffles—Zoe's pug—jumped onto the table.

"What's up? Do the two of you want to join the team too?" asked Tim.

The two pets wagged their tails happily. **BARF! WOOF!**

Zoe giggled.

"In that case, we should also invite Dr. Curtis!" Tito requested on behalf of his pet iguana.

"And Margot!" added Tim.

"Okay, how many are we, then?" asked Tito, using his fingers to count.

"I have a suggestion," said Zoe. "Why don't we call ourselves the Justice Friends instead? That way there will always be room for others to join!"

It was a terrific idea. "Let's do it!" shouted Tim.

"Perfect, so now that that's taken care of, we can move to our last item of business," declared Tito, standing up. "Tim, on behalf of the Justice Friends, I'd like to congratulate you for harnessing the power of your worries for the first time ever!"

Tito wrapped Tim in a bear hug, while Zoe and Oskar burst into applause. "Tim! Tim! Tim!" the three of them chanted.

Tim's cheeks were burning, and he didn't know where to look. "Thank you . . . I mean, I doubt I can do it again, though. It was a fluke."

"Well, there's only one way to find out, right?" asked Tito, patting Tim's shoulder.

Tim nodded, and Oskar jumped out of his seat.

"Then what are we waiting for?" Oskar asked.

You see, Tim's life was complicated, and unexpected, and often dangerous and messy, too.

But among all that uncertainty, Tim had learned that one thing was for sure: no matter what happened, he wasn't on his own.

ACKNOWLEDGMENTS

This book wouldn't have been possible without the love and support of my wonderful wife, head cheerleader, and best friend: Jacko. I want to thank my children, too, for being the best kids in the whole multiverse. Andrea, I'm so proud that you want to follow my steps and become a writer and illustrator. It's not an easy path, but with your talent and drive, I'm sure you can achieve whatever you set out to do. Adrian, every time I see you with a book in your hands, laughing, I feel like breaking into a happy dance. Thank you for being the best board game buddy ever, and for making me want to become a better writer! Thanks also to my parents, Eni and Francisco, for their unconditional love and for always believing in me.

Thanks to my friends in Spain, Hong Kong, the USA, and many other places around the world. I feel incredibly lucky to know you all, and I'm forever grateful for all your support. Please keep sending me pics and videos of your kids reading Tim Possible. I love them!

Thanks to the team at the Bent Agency and in particular to my agent, Gemma Cooper. Thanks for having my back, and for being there anytime I need it. You make my life 1,000 percent easier. Go, Team Cooper!

Thanks to my wonderful editors, Karen Nagel and Jessi Smith. Thanks again for believing in me and for giving me this opportunity to develop Tim's story. It's always a pleasure working with you, and I suggest that you keep an eye on your inbox because book 4 is shaping up to be epic! Thanks to Karin Paprocki for your guidance in bringing my characters to life and for helping me become a better illustrator. Thanks also to Mike Rosamilia, Amelia Jenkins, Valerie Shea, Bara MacNeill, Chel Morgan, Lauren Forte, and the rest of the Aladdin/Simon & Schuster team. Even though I don't get to work with you directly, I know that without each and every one of you, this book wouldn't have been possible. You have my endless thanks!

I'd also like to thank the wonderful Marin Horizon Community, and in particular the talented lower-school artists who helped me create the illustration for part 3 of this book. You rock! Thanks also to my Mill Valley and Marin County neighbors for their kindness and support.

Finally, thanks to you, the reader. This story, and all the hard work it took to create it, is meaningless without you. I hope you enjoyed reading this book as much as I enjoyed writing and illustrating it, and I hope you'll continue to join me, Tim, Tito, and Oskar on this wonderful journey. You'll see, book 4 is going to be legendary. ¡Muchas gracias!

ABOUT THE AUTHOR

AXEL MAISY was born and raised in Barcelona and has lived most of his adult life in Hong Kong. He currently lives in Mill Valley, California, surrounded by magnificent redwood forests with lovely hiking trails that he wishes he'd visit more often. When he is not writing or drawing big-eyed characters, Axel spends his time watching squirrels and unsuccessfully chasing raccoons away from his vegetable garden.